JOHAN TWISS

I
AM
SLEEPLESS
SIM 299

I AM
SLEEPLESS
SIM 299

Johan Twiss

Twiss Publishing, Copyright © 2015
by John A. Burger (pen name Johan Twiss)
All rights reserved.
Editor: Heather B. Monson
Cover Illustrator: Sky Young
Interior Sketches: Adrienne Burger
Proofreader: Kent Meyers
Proofreader: Ken Meyers
ISBN-13: 978-1517166335
ISBN-10: 1517166330

DEDICATION

To N, L, C, J & H.
The fiercest, funniest, smartest, craziest,
and cutest prime cadets I know.

JOIN THE CLUB!

I hope you'll join the JT Reader Club to get the latest freebies, discounts, and exclusives on upcoming stories and events.

The JT is for Johan Twiss. Not sure how to pronounce my first name? Just pretend you saw Han Solo from Star Wars and said, "Yo, Han. What's up?"

There, you've got it!

Go to www.johantwiss.com to join the club today!

PRIME ABILITIES & DEFECTS

VIBRUNT [vibe-runt] – (Green)

ABILITY: Vibrunts are able to feel and hear sound and radio waves and to create 3D images of their surroundings in their minds.

DEFECT: Vibrunts are permanently blind. They lose the use of their eyesight once they are administered the Prime Injection.

PUZZLER [puzz-ler] – (Gray)

ABILITY: Puzzlers can solve complex equations, puzzles, and programming. They can often do this faster than quire processors as their minds absorb and sort massive amounts of data simultaneously, rather than processing it in a string of code like a quire processor does.

DEFECT: The puzzler defect, commonly known as "the shakes," causes involuntary muscle spasms throughout their body. Their muscles contract rapidly, causing small tremors and twitches to shake them uncontrollably. The non-stop shaking makes it difficult for puzzlers to sleep, eat, and work. Most puzzlers die by the age of five due to the stress on their bodies.

EIDETIC [eye-de-tic] – (Brown)

ABILITY: Eidetics have a photographic memory with perfect recall for anything they have seen or read. They are exceptionally fast readers and they are physically stronger than all other primes, except lugs, due to their size.

DEFECT: Eidetics are plagued by gigantism. Their bodies never stop growing until they die, which is usually due to heart failure. This non-stop growth causes non-stop pain as their bones, muscles, and joints continually expand. Most eidetics don't live past age forty.

AGULATOR [ag-u-late-or] – (White)
ABILITY: Agulators are able to change the weight of their bodies. This allows them to become as light as a feather and float in the air, or to become extremely heavy like a hippophant.
DEFECT: Agulators are extremely allergic to UV rays from the sun. When any part of their flesh is exposed, it burns rapidly as if on fire. For this reason, all agulators wear protective gear that covers them from head to toe. As a precautionary rule, they rarely remove this protective gear, even indoors.

MEK [mehk] – (Blue)
ABILITY: Meks are genius engineers and tech builders. Their minds work similarly to a puzzler's, but in the narrowly focused area of engineering and inventing. They are naturally skilled with tools and programming for the tech they create.
DEFECT: Meks are unique in that they manifest two defects. The first is dwarfism. The average height for a fully grown mek is three feet five inches tall. They also subconsciously sabotage any tech they create with their own hands so others cannot use it.

LUG [lug] – (Gold)

ABILITY: Lugs are gifted with super strength, a tougher muscular-skeletal structure, and an epidermis that can handle great amounts of stress and impact.

DEFECT: The lug defect is muteness. Although their vocal chords appear to be perfectly intact, there is an unknown disconnect from their brain to their vocal chords that prohibits them from speaking vocally.

VIGORI [vi-gore-e] – (Red)

ABILITY: Vigori have super speed and agility. Their increased metabolism also allows them to heal at an accelerated rate, when provided enough nourishment.

DEFECT: Vigori must have constant food and water to survive. If a vigori goes without eating or drinking for more than twelve hours, they die.

READER [read-er] – (Orange)

ABILITY: Unknown to the general public.

DEFECT: Unknown to the general public.

ALL PRIMES

ABILITY: All primes are immune from infection by the Splicers and cannot be turned into Splicers themselves. This is why they are at the front lines of the Splicer War.

DEFECT: Primes are unable to produce offspring with other primes. They must marry and mate humans to produce offspring. This also strengthens the human gene pool for those compatible with the Prime Stimulus.

CHAPTER 1: THE PIT

I have come to believe that there is no escape from war. The only solution is to control it. Control is key, and the Prime Initiative offers that control. It is the only way to save our worlds. Hashmeer is overtaken and soon Omori and Ethos will fall. Even if I could sleep, I would fear the nightmares that are coming for us.

—Doctor T.M. Omori,
Man's Quest for Destruction: A Case for the Prime Initiative

Do you really think he is the key to ending this war?" General Estrago asked. "He is just a boy. True, he possesses two rare gifts, but I do not see how they translate into victory on the battlefield."

Director Tuskin flared his nostrils in annoyance. "Estrago, in all of my lifetimes he is the only other prime, besides myself, born with multiple gifts and without defects. Despite your benighted observations, his two rare gifts are the most important to our cause. Not even I am a puzzler or a vibrunt."

General Estrago shifted his bulk to the left side and winced as a painful crack emanated from his lower back. The thick protruding scars on his face tightened as he clenched his jaw against the pain. The scars zig-zagged from his forehead, down his dark brown face, through his neatly-trimmed beard, and crept down his neck like a spidergoose web, until they disappeared beneath the high brown collar of his uniform.

He had grown another three inches in the last year and stood over ten feet tall, but the pain was becoming unbearable. He wondered how much longer his body would hold out. Few eidetics lived to his age—even fewer grew to his stature. General Estrago waited another moment for the shooting pain to dissipate before continuing.

"He is unique. No other puzzler on record has lived past the age of eight. He will be twelve next week and will join the upper coteries in the trials, but only three of their original twelve coterie members remain. They are the youngest and smallest group in the trials. They do not have a chance in the Pit."

Director Tuskin stared at the image of Aidan on the holovid.

"Thank you for your input, Estrago. What you don't realize is that I've been slimming down his coterie over these last few years for this very purpose."

"You have?" General Estrago questioned, alarmed by the revelation. "But they were only children, sir, let alone prime cadets. We need all the primes we can train for the war."

Director Tuskin dismissed the accusation with a wave of his hand.

"You forget your place, Estrago. You forget who I am. You forget what I did to your coterie when you were a boy."

General Estrago paled. He closed his eyes to block the memories and subconsciously ran his fingers along the web of scars on his face.

Director Tuskin rose from his chair and walked to the holovid, his face inches away from the image of Aidan.

"Everything I do is for the survival of this planet. Ethos and the human race cannot be wiped out. We must continue to push this boy to develop his gifts. If I am right, he is the key to ending this war."

***

"DUCK!" Aidan yelled into his commlink.

Fig dove backward, watching in horror as a boulder the size of a bipod flew overhead.

"Thanks," Fig trembled, sweat beading along his blue forehead. "I didn't see it coming."

"No problem. I can hear their whole coterie on the other side of the ridge. Four lugs, two meks, two agulators, and one eidetic."

"Tuskin's fury!" Fig swore. "Remind me how this is fair? Nine fifteen-year cadets against the three of us. We're so dead. And this sun is absolutely blinding me."

Aidan dashed behind a destroyed bipod. Smoke rose from the towering heap of the crashed hover vehicle as it lay amongst the goblin-like pillars of red stone protruding from the canyon floor. The shadows cast by the bipod's crunched, burnt metal camouflaged his own gray skin and his gray and green uniform, but it did little to hide his bright green hair and one bright green eye.

"Relax, Fig," Aidan said between breaths. "This is what we've trained for since we were kids. Now we have a chance to test our skills against other cadets. Plus, we have an advantage."

"We do?"

"Yeah. I just stepped in bearcat dung," Aidan said with a grin.

"What? Gross. How is smelling like you haven't showered in a month an advantage? We're so dead. Dead, I tell you. Dead. Dead. Dead."

"Fig. Calm down. I also know where they're hiding their trophy and they have no clue where to find ours."

Aidan bent over and touched the ground. Closing his eyes to concentrate, he used his gift as a vibrunt to vibroscan the Pit, focusing his mind to feel the pulses in the earth and listen to the air waves around the surrounding canyon. A multi-dimensional image of the battlefield came clearly to his mind. On the far end of the wide canyon stood the fifteen-year prime base, protected by a natural wall of red rock with jutting spires along the wall edge.

"They're taking a defensive position," Aidan said. "I think they're testing us before attacking. They've never fought a coterie like ours."

"You mean they've never faced a prime like you."

Aidan nodded, though Fig couldn't see him. He knew he freaked out all the upper coteries. They hid their fear through the usual name calling, insults, and unfriendly hand gestures back in Mount Fegorio.

A distinct tapping, their private comms code, echoed in their earpieces.

"I read you, Palomas," Aidan said. "You're right. We need to draw them out. Ideas, anyone?"

"I say we throw them our trophy and call it a day," Fig answered.

"Better idea," Palomas tapped into her earpiece. "Fig jumps into their base shooting fireballs and then runs away like a baby."

Aidan chuckled.

"No!" Fig complained. "That's a horrible idea. In the history of ideas that is the worst. I may have the awesomest mek suit ever, but all nine of them would smash me into nanobits."

"You're such a wuss," Palomas tapped. "They can't really kill you."

Fig huffed. "I know that. But remember what General Estrago always preaches: 'If you break a leg during the trial it will feel like you broke your leg in real life.' Which means if you die in a trial you get all the pain of death. I'll pass, thanks."

"She does have a point," Aidan countered. "We need a distraction and your suit makes you the fastest. They also won't leave the base unguarded with Palomas still hiding in the canyon. So here's what we do."

Aidan quickly laid out a plan and promised Fig his dessert ration if he would cooperate.

For such a tiny mek, he eats as much as a lug, Aidan thought. "Okay, everyone ready?"

"No!" Fig exclaimed.

"Perfect—let's go," Palomas tapped.

Palomas darted from her hiding spot against the canyon wall to hide behind a pile of large boulders in view of the enemy base. Her rich golden skin and long golden hair, pulled back in a tight bun, sparkled in the sunlight. Her matching golden uniform of the Ethos army left no mistake that she was a lug.

"How far away?" Palomas tapped.

"About 500 feet. Think you can make it that far?"

Palomas rolled her eyes and heaved one of the massive rocks toward the enemy. It hit the ridge wall of the enemy base and the crash echoed throughout the Pit.

"Nice! You got their attention, but now aim ten feet to the left and fifteen feet higher," Aidan called.

He vibroscanned, watching as Palomas tossed the next giant boulder into the heart of the enemy base. Aidan cringed when the boulder crushed two of the opposing coterie, taking them out of the trial game.

"They're down one lug and an agulator. And they look mad. You're up, Fig."

From the cockpit of his mek suit, Fig adjusted his sweaty hands on the controls. They turned a lighter shade of blue as he squeezed the control sticks tighter.

"You are the man. You can do this. Breathe," he whispered to himself.

"Fig! Go now, you little blue midget!" Palomas tapped impatiently. "A lug and an agulator jumped the wall and are on my tail."

Letting out a final breath, Fig stepped out from his hiding place behind a giant red boulder. He stood on a long platform of red rock about forty feet up the canyon wall. The feet of his mek suit gripped the sandstone rock as he dashed toward the edge of the cliff, yelled a war cry, and jumped. Fig looked out his mek suit window in awe as he soared through the air in a wide arc. To his surprise, and relief, he landed safely in the main clearing at the center of the canyon. With nowhere to hide, he took off at a sprint toward the enemy base.

"Can I just say that I hate both of you right now?" he shouted over the hum of his exoskeleton mek battle suit.

"Noted." Aidan answered. "Palomas, be careful. There's a second lug on your left trying to flank you."

"Got it," Palomas tapped while dodging a boulder.

Approaching at full speed, Fig lifted his mek suit arms and shot two fireballs toward the ridge wall surrounding the enemy base. It exploded in flames, sending a lug sprawling backward. Two enemy meks emerged, jumping over the ridge. They fired a round of mist rockets at Fig, creating a smokescreen that spread out across the center of the canyon.

A harpoon, with a chain attached to it, shot through the smoke directly at Fig's chest.

Fig barely dodged the first projectile when a second harpoon struck him in the right leg of his suit, exploding into a gooey mess which hardened in seconds.

"Spidergeese!" Fig swore. "They're using plaster rounds, Aidan. They don't want to kill me. They want to capture my suit, steal my tech, and then kill me."

"I figured they might," Aidan replied. "Keep them busy. I'm almost in their base. They were nice to create that smokescreen for me to sneak in."

Fig swore again as the other mek landed a second plaster round to his torso. The two enemy meks began retracting their chains to reel him in.

Oh no you don't, Fig thought, pushing the button labeled 'Lug-Mode' on his control panel. The hum of his suit dropped deeper as the torque increased throughout its limbs. Lug-Mode was one of his newest upgrades. It made the suit sluggish, but incredibly strong. He wasn't quite as strong as Palomas when he went into Lug-Mode, but he was pretty close.

Gripping both of the attached chains, Fig yanked. Before they could react, the surprised enemy meks found themselves being dragged across the ground like play toys.

"Way to go, Fig!" Palomas tapped. The smoke began to clear and Palomas came into view on the opposite side of the base. She raced toward Fig with three enemy primes close behind.

"Hope you don't mind. I'm bringing my friends over to play."

Aidan smiled as he watched the scene unfold. This was turning out better than he had expected. Slipping over the southernmost part of the enemy wall, he landed softly in their base. He vibroscanned the area, taking note of the agulator and two lugs lying on the ground, already taken out by Fig and Palomas.

All I have to do is get by the eidetic, Aidan thought, spying the seven-foot-tall, dark brown eidetic teenager guarding the trophy.

He felt bad for eidetics. Their size and photographic recall were amazing, but they never stopped growing. This did make them stronger than all the other primes, besides lugs, but the non-stop growth led to excruciating non-stop growing pains. It was the eidetic defect.

Pushing his sympathy aside, Aidan crept closer to the eidetic and reached into his pants pocket, removing a bag full of the bearcat dung he had stepped in earlier.

I feel sorry for this guy, Aidan thought. Taking off his pack, he gingerly reached inside and retrieved another bag, but this one was full of burning beetlants.

"Glad I found your nest in the cave," Aidan whispered to the tiny insects. "Hopefully my aim is as good as Palomas'."

Aidan opened the bag full of sloppy, noxious bearcat dung, stood from his hiding place, and threw it at the eidetic.

Splat! The dung found its mark.

"Why, you little twerp!" the eidetic bellowed as he lumbered toward Aidan. The eidetic's dark brown uniform and dark brown skin made him look like a walking tree trunk as he approached.

Aidan shook his head sorrowfully. "Hey, man, for what it's worth, I really am sorry about this. It's just a trial game, okay." He opened the second bag and tossed the burning beetlants at the eidetic's feet.

"You missed," the eidetic boy sneered.

Aidan frowned. "No, I didn't."

The beetlants, now released from the bag, caught a whiff of the bearcat dung and swarmed. The poor boy swung his hands in futile attempts to swat them away, but it was no use. Hundreds of tiny beetlants bit and bored into his skin, leaving fiery red welts and pinpricks of brown blood in their wake, causing the boy to collapse to the ground unconscious.

"I'm really sorry about this," Aidan muttered again, feeling sick as he walked past eidetic boy on his way toward the trophy.

He reached out to grab the thin trophy disc, but stopped. Puzzler mode took over. Something was wrong.

It's a trap, his mind spat out. *The two lugs and the agulator are faking their injuries, and the trophy on display is a counterfeit. The real trophy is with one of the meks in the center of the Pit.*

"Tuskin's fury!" Aidan swore into his commlink. "Palomas, Fig, the trophy is with one of their meks. You've got to find it now!"

No answer.

"Fig? Palomas? Do you hear me?"

Aidan felt vibrations in the air and dove to the side as a boulder flew toward him from behind.

"Lucky move, punk," the agulator taunted as she floated through the air toward Aidan. Her white facemask and billowing white cloak gave the agulator an eerie appearance of an angel floating in the air.

An angel of death, Aidan thought.

The two golden-skinned lugs skulked behind the agulator, each carrying massive rocks.

"Since my two lug brothers can't speak, let me tell you how this is going to work, you two-toned freak. You tell us where your trophy is hidden and I will kill you quickly. No pain."

"Fig? Palomas?" Aidan whispered.

The Agulator smiled. "Oh, our meks jammed your commlink," she said matter-of-factly. "I have to say, though, for your first trial you losers did better than expected. But even with your freak powers, you never had a chance."

What to do? thought Aidan as he stared at the approaching agulator.

The agulator changed her weight and came crashing to the ground with the force of a meteor, leaving a small crater.

"Time's up, freak. Tell me where your trophy is."

Aidan felt the trophy under his shirt, secured to his chest with the special vest he made to hide books that General Estrago, the headmaster of Mount Fegorio, smuggled to him each week. The small metal disc felt cold and tingled against his warm skin. It was an exact copy of the real trophy discs used to power all the war machines of the Ethos military. But these trophy discs were mere replicas and held no power charge.

Maybe keeping the trophy with me wasn't such a good idea after all, Aidan thought.

"Okay, I'll tell you," Aidan said, trembling and feigning panic. "I'll tell you where the trophy is, but you don't have to kill any of us. Just keep me here, go get the trophy, and you win."

The white agulator half-floated, half-stepped her way to stand directly in front of Aidan. She settled to the ground gracefully this time as she slowly changed her weight.

I wonder if she's pretty under that mask, Aidan thought.

Agulators rarely took their masks off in public. He could use his vibrant powers to see under her mask, but he would never try it. His instructor, Captain Solsti, had ingrained in him to respect others privacy with his powers, and he had.

Aidan had only seen one agulator's face before—a girl in their coterie named Mesqule. Aidan remembered her happy, beautiful, snow-white face. But sadly, Mesqule died last year, and the deadly female agulator standing before him was definitely not Mesqule. This was Kara, captain of the fifteen-year primes, and she had hated Aidan for as long as he could remember.

"*Shhh*," Kara whispered. "I'm not going to hurt you…much."

Pulling back her arm, she punched Aidan square in the chest, changing the weight of her arm to that of a war hammer. As Aidan tumbled flat on his back, the two lugs let out breathy laughs, though no sound came out. Muteness was the lug defect.

Luckily the trophy strapped to his chest took the brunt of Kara's blow, but Aidan knew his ribs were definitely bruised, if not broken.

Changing to the weight of a feather, Kara jumped up and floated above Aidan while he lay on his back gasping for air.

"You have until the count of three before I let myself fall down on you with the weight of a hippophant."

"ONE."

I'm so dead, Aidan thought.

"TWO."

If I give her the trophy, she'll just kill me anyway and their coterie will get more points for collecting our trophy.

"THREE"

Aidan closed his eyes, preparing to be squashed.

"Time's up freak. Enjoy your first death in the Pit."

Aidan's eyes snapped open, his senses heightened like never before. He felt his mind and body meld between vibruntcy and puzzler mode in a new way he had never experienced.

Kara came crashing down, but Aidan rolled to the side at precisely the right moment to avoid her smashing assault.

His mind cleared and focused acutely on the world around him. Everything seemed to move in slow-motion as he processed every minute detail of his surroundings. He ran toward the lugs as they heaved jagged rocks at him, easily sidestepping their throws. He knew exactly where their throws would land before they released them.

Recovering from her miss, Kara turned, ran a few steps to build up momentum and then jumped, changing her weight to rocket toward Aidan. With his back turned to Kara, Aidan dodged the deadly punches of the lugs, then sidestepped as Kara changed her weight to smash into him. But instead of hitting Aidan, she flattened one of her brother lugs.

Aidan's stomach churned as he heard the lug's bones break under the weight of the agulator.

Fuming, Kara rushed at Aidan, swinging ferociously. She jumped in the air, flying around him while she attacked from multiple angles. Aidan easily dodged her punches and those of the remaining lug. In one swift movement, he slipped his arm through Kara's defenses and grabbed her fastened mask in just the right spot to swipe it off her head. The agulator screamed as

the sun's rays burned her exposed pale white flesh and
she used her hands to cover her face.

UV rays, Aidan thought sadly. *The agulator defect.*

Sensing the lug approaching from behind, Aidan
calculated the perfect movement to guide the lug's swing
directly into Kara's path. A resounding crack filled the air
as the lug's fist connected with the Kara's skull, sending
her down for good. The surprised lug bent over his sister,
shocked by what he had done and terrified as he watched
her exposed milky white face sizzle in the sunlight.

With Kara out of the trial, Aidan scrambled to the
top of the ridge wall and took one last look at the
remaining lug.

"Sorry about all this," he called back sincerely,
waving his hand in the direction of the lug's fallen
comrades. He really was sorry they had to fight, but he
knew he needed to taunt the lug for his plan to work and
to save Fig and Palomas.

"Just remember," Aidan said with a wink of his gray
eye. "You were the one who hit her, not me. Hopefully
Kara will forgive your clumsiness." Aidan smiled and
winked his green eye this time.

The lug's face flushed a deep gold. He grabbed a
nearby boulder, just as Aidan knew he would, and heaved
it at Aidan with all his strength. Aidan's mind precisely
judged everything as he took a running start, jumped off
the ridge toward the oncoming boulder, and landed safely
on top of it as it flew like a bipod flyer into the sky.

Aidan rode the aerial boulder toward the center of
the Pit where Fig and Palomas fought for their virtual

lives. Aidan's weight sent the trajectory of the boulder careening toward one of the meks Fig was fighting. Just before it collided with the mek, Aidan jumped off the boulder with a graceful tuck-and-roll.

The projectile smashed the mek suit hatch open, revealing a tiny, three-foot-tall blue mek at the controls. Next to him lay the trophy.

Aidan scrambled to the disc and grabbed it. Immediately their virtual surroundings changed from the bright blue sky and rocky red terrain of the canyon to multiple rows of trainer seats lined at the front of a spacious assembly hall with dozens of spectators. They had survived their first trial competition in the Pit.

BURNING BEETLANT

CHAPTER 2: SLEEPLESS

One downside to never sleeping is that I never dream. My mind never escapes reality. While everyone else sleeps and escapes, I work. I read. I plan. Such is my fate as the first Prime.

—Doctor T.M. Omori,
Man's Quest for Destruction: A Case for the Prime Initiative

A idan blinked as the assembly hall came into focus. The tall metal walls of the large room spanned all three floors of the Mount Fegorio complex. A half-circle of stadium seats rose high above a small circular stage where Aidan, Fig, Palomas, and their opposing fifteen-year coterie were now unharnessing from their trainer seats.

Displayed above their heads, a massive thirty-foot holovid replayed highlights from the trial, showing Aidan riding a boulder as it flew into the opposing mek with the trophy. The spectators in the assembly hall stood stunned as this highlight, along with those of Aidan easily dodging multiple attacks, played over and over.

During the trial, the giant holovid provided a live feed to the action in the simulation. Prime cadets and other staff at Mount Fegorio gathered in the assembly hall to watch coteries battle. Viewpoints from each participant were shown in separate boxes on the holovid in addition to three wide-angle aerial views of the canyon. This allowed the cadets to view, critique, and learn from the battle strategy successes and failures of their fellow cadets.

Aidan unstrapped his headband harness and unhooked his quire processor from the trainer seat. He sat up to find Fig and Palomas already unharnessed and standing at his side, grinning ear-to-ear.

"I can't believe we did it!" Fig shouted much too loudly. His voice echoed off the metal walls of the assembly hall while the rest of the spectators, including cadets, the master instructors and the support staff, were whispering to each other in hushed tones.

"You guys were awesome!" Palomas signed with her hands, then brought Aidan and Fig in for a bone-crushing hug. She let go, then signed, "We'd better go give our debriefing statements to General Estrago."

"Yeah," Fig agreed, still smiling with excitement. "Let's hurry, because I'm starving! Plus, I want to watch the trial replays back in Aidan's room."

Aidan returned their beaming smiles but said nothing. Although he was excited that they survived their first head-to-head trial, he was still trying to grasp what had happened with his powers. He tried once again to turn on puzzler mode. He focused, pushed and prodded his mind.

Nothing, he thought.

He focused his vibruntcy, and immediately a 3D image of his surroundings popped into his mind.

At least that still works.

His vibruntcy caught a glimpse of Kara as she unharnessed from her trainer seat. Her beautiful face turned ugly as it contorted into a glaring sneer that followed Aidan's every move—at least that's what he imagined she looked like behind the mask.

Aidan shut off his vibruntcy and tried to ignore her, but he still felt her stare burning into his back.

"I can't believe we just won! Can you believe it? I can't!" Fig rambled on excitedly as the trio walked off the stage and trekked up the long aisle of stairs rising to the exit doors of the assembly hall.

A few of the younger primes congratulated them and stared at Aidan in awe as he passed. The majority of the other spectators kept their distance, still whispering quietly about what they had just witnessed.

Aidan felt a painful shove to his left shoulder, sending him flying into the back of Palomas, who then toppled awkwardly over Fig.

"Hey! Watch it!" Fig shouted from underneath Palomas.

Aidan turned to see the cause of his fall and found the sixteen-year senior agulator, Dixon, standing above him.

"Sorry about that," Dixon said sharply. He extended a hand towards Aidan. "I didn't see you there. Let me help you up."

Aidan cautiously offered Dixon his hand. The senior agulator squeezed it tightly and yanked Aidan upwards until he was mere inches from Dixon's facemask.

"You'll pay for what you did to Kara in the trial. Watch your back, freak," Dixon hissed in a barely audible whisper. Gently pushing Aidan away, he roughly patted Aidan on the back and spoke in a much louder tone for all to hear. "There. No harm done. Congrats on your first trial win, Aidan."

Aidan narrowed his green and gray eyes as he stared up at the much taller and much stronger senior prime.

"No harm done to me, though I'm more worried about you," Aidan replied with a hint of sarcasm. "I didn't realize you were so clumsy. You should watch your step more carefully. A clumsy agulator can be quite dangerous to his coterie."

"Why, you little…who are you calling clumsy?" Dixon hissed.

Having successfully untangled herself from Fig, Palomas stood at Aidan's side and glared at Dixon.

"Let's go," she signed to Aidan. "I'm clumsy myself sometimes. I'd hate to trip and accidentally crush a nearby agulator's shoulder when I grabbed it for support. That would be such a pity."

Dixon went silent, turned his back to them, and headed down the stairs toward Kara.

***

"I can hardly believe what the boy did," General Estrago said in his seat across from Director Tuskin.

The Director huffed. "And you said his skills would be pointless in battle."

"I did not call them pointless," General Estrago corrected. "What I said was that 'he possesses two rare gifts, but I do not see how they translate into victory on the battlefield.'"

The Director slammed his hand against the table. His skin flashed white and he floated menacingly in the air above General Estrago as his agulator powers took hold. "Don't correct me with your high-and-mighty eidetic accuracies, fool. I was an eidetic long before you, and my memories span centuries."

General Estrago slumped in his chair. He had worked for the Director all his life, learning to navigate his temper and read his mannerisms. Even though he was now the general of Mount Fegorio and had reached the ripe age of forty, he still feared the Director's wrath.

General Estrago bowed his head and tugged at the high collar of his brown uniform. It seemed to constrict his neck under the intense stare of the Director. "Sir, I apologize. Please forgive me."

Director Tuskin landed softly back in his chair and waved a dismissive hand. "Oh, stop sniveling, you oversized brute, and tell me what Aidan said after the trial. You spoke with him, correct?"

General Estrago nodded and straightened his broad shoulders, attempting to regain his composure. "Yes, we just finished his debriefing. He said he wasn't sure what happened. His powers melded on their own. His vibruntcy and puzzler abilities became one. As a trained doctor and scientist, I hypothesize that it allowed him to calculate his movements and actions precisely to achieve his desired outcome."

"Interesting. Can he do it at will?"

General Estrago shook his head. "According to him, no. He tried after the trial, but nothing. He said puzzler mode just happens and he's never melded it with his vibruntcy before."

"Almost like an instinctual response to his life being threatened. We need to help him master his melding."

"How do you propose we accomplish that, sir?"

Director Tuskin's skin flashed brown and his eyes narrowed as he racked through centuries of his own eidetic memories. "For now, give him an extra session with Captain Solsti. I will ponder on the matter more and decide our course of action."

General Estrago's brown cheeks blushed a darker brown at the mention of Captain Solsti. His own eidetic mind replayed through dozens of fond memories with the woman and fellow teacher. Catching himself, he quickly turned his thoughts back to Director Tuskin and resumed thinking like the trained doctor and scientist he was. Nearly all eidetics became doctors, scientists and medics for the Ethos Army. Their gift of perfect recall granted them a unique advantage in those fields. It also created a penchant for curiosity, similar to that of a puzzler.

"I wonder," General Estrago asked. "Has this ever happened to you, Director? Have your powers melded before?"

The Director stared at his hands as they began to tremble. He did not answer.

***

After their debriefings with General Estrago, Aidan, Fig, and Palomas hurried to Aidan's room and sat glued to the holovid, rewatching their first trial.

"I still don't understand," Palomas signed with her hands, after watching the trial for the fifth time. "How did you do that? You were unstoppable. It's like you were more than a prime."

"Like I told General Estrago, I don't know what happened. It was strange. My gifts kind of melded together. I saw everything in my mind and all the data points connected to calculate the outcomes. It was almost like I could see into the future and knew exactly how to make it work in my favor."

"Batmonkeys, that's weird," Fig swore.

Aidan nodded, trying to understand it himself. He had trouble explaining puzzler mode to others. Few prime cadets became puzzlers and most died as infants, due to their defect of uncontrollable shaking—but he was different. He had no defects.

He also had no control over puzzler mode. It just happened. Without notice, he could tell the innermost secrets of a person. What food they liked, hidden illnesses, hobbies, fears, and personal secrets came rushing to his mind. Math, computing, riddles—all the same. But he had no control over the gift. Puzzler mode came on sporadically, like a gust of wind, and would provide him answers. He didn't always understand how he knew the answers—and often he didn't know there was a problem that needed solving—but if all of the data points became available, his mind assembled them together like an intricate puzzle to provide a solution.

DONG - DONG - DONG. The Mount Fegorio complex bell rang three times, signaling lights out and time for bed.

"Well, I hope you can do it again on the next trial," Palomas signed, putting down the brush she was using to untangle her long golden hair before going to bed. As a soldier, she kept it in a tight bun during the day, but longed to let it go free each night.

"Anyways," Palomas continued, "I'm off to my room. Good night, losers. I love you guys."

Aidan smiled. Since his first memories formed of them learning to communicate as one-year primes, Palomas had signed the same thing to their coterie family every night, *Good night, losers. I love you.*

"Love you too, sis," replied Fig and Aidan in unison.

Although they were not blood related, they had been raised together since receiving the Prime Injection as newborn infants. After losing the rest of their coterie members to death and illness, Aidan, Fig and Palomas were all the family they knew.

Fig jumped off his chair to follow Palomas out the door and head to his own room. The short blue mek stood nearly three feet tall and only came to just above Palomas' and Aidan's belly buttons as he stood to leave.

"See you tomorrow, bro," Fig said. "Don't do anything tonight I wouldn't do."

Aidan waved goodnight to Fig and Palomas as they left. The door slid closed behind them and he rolled over on his bed, gazing at his empty room. Though small, his room had everything he needed—a bed, a desk, a wash room, and his personal trainer seat.

The walls were a bleak, metallic gray with no decorations, like the rest of the Mount Fegorio complex. But that didn't bother Aidan. The color gray suited him just fine, since he was covered head-to-toe in light gray skin. This created an odd juxtaposition with his mop of thick green hair, which tended to stand straight up. These were the mixed colors of a gray puzzler and a green vibrunt. Even his eyes were mixed, with one a stoic gray color and the other a brilliant green.

To Aidan, his colors made him unique. There was no one else like him in Mount Fegorio. The closest was Captain Solsti, one of the master instructors. She was the only other vibrunt at this complex—very rare, and an oddity with her green skin, green hair, and the vibrunt defect of blindness. She walked around the complex with her eyes closed, using vibruntcy to see, and had trained Aidan to control his gift since it first manifested at the age of two.

Puzzler mode manifested itself shortly after his vibruntcy, causing quite a stir throughout Mount Fegorio. No one had seen a prime with two gifts, let alone a puzzler without the shakes. When Aidan's unique defect first appeared, General Estrago removed Aidan from the rest of his coterie, giving him his own room so that he would not distract the others at night.

Why am I even lying in bed? Aidan thought. *It's not like I'm going to fall asleep.*

It wasn't the excitement of their first win in the trials, his upcoming new upper-coterie classes for the year, or the vague threats from Dixon that kept him awake.

The fact of the matter was that Aidan never slept.

That was his defect, if you could call it one. To Aidan, this was his third gift.

Rolling off the bed, he grabbed his quire processor and attached it to his wrist. With a few taps on the quire screen he dimmed the lights in his room and sent the hidden cameras onto a pre-programmed loop. No one else in the complex knew about the hidden cameras in all the rooms, except Fig and Palomas, of course. Aidan told them right away, and they were good at keeping secrets.

He was eight when he discovered the cameras by happenstance while randomly going into puzzler mode. At the size of a freckle, the cameras were nearly invisible. Every room in the Mount Fegorio complex, from the dorms to classrooms, held hidden cameras. One night, puzzler mode took over his mind. Not only did it detect the cameras, but it sent him into a feverish fury of code hacking on his quire processor. He didn't really understand everything he was doing, but somehow he turned his quire into a key to the complex.

With his room cameras on a loop that showed Aidan playing games and wandering around his room, he tapped his quire to unlock his doors. No alarms sounded.

"Let's see what's going on in Fegorio tonight," he whispered.

Switching on his vibruntcy, Aidan searched for signs of movement in the main corridor as he passed the area designated for cadet sleeping quarters. Fig and Palomas each had their own rooms next to his. Most coteries shared large dormitory rooms, one for the boys and one for the girls. Not them. Palomas was the only girl left since Mesqule died one year prior, and Fig got his own room after Chauncy's death.

Aidan turned off the cameras and alarms as he continued down the hallway toward the commissary. While others slept with no need for food, his body required a second dinner to make it through the night.

Fig had come with him on his night walks a few times before, eager to swipe an extra meal from the food printers, but he was always drained and could barely keep his eyelids open the next day. For Aidan, it was part of his nightly routine and no one ever noticed—no one but General Estrago, the Mount Fegorio headmaster and Warfare History instructor. The man seemed to be everywhere and caught Aidan one night in the middle of printing a meat pie.

Aidan entered the commissary undetected and connected his quire to one of the food printers. Soon he was scarfing down warm biscuits with honey, fruit gelatin and a small stack of sweet cakes. He printed a few extra sweet cakes to share with Fig and Palomas in the morning. Before reentering the hallway, he paused at the door.

Right on time, he thought as a lug security team passed by. The security patrols were never tardy and kept an exact schedule at Mount Fegorio. Luckily for Aidan, their precision made it easier for him to move around at night.

Once clear, Aidan made a series of turns from the main hallway and climbed a set of stairs to the third level where the masters resided.

Over the past two years, he had explored nearly all of the gray, metal hallways of the massive Mount Fegorio complex. The complex was simple to navigate, since it ran in a giant one-mile ring along the outer ridge of a dormant volcano. There were three levels to the complex, with a main hallway running in a full circle on each level. If you ever got lost on a level, all you had to do was find the main corridor and keep walking in a circle until you made your way back to a place you knew.

While the master instructors resided on the third level top floor, security and general staff occupied the bottom level. The young cadets, ages newborn to sixteen, kept to the second level, where all of their sleeping quarters, classrooms, and the commissary were located. The only differing room was the giant assembly hall, which spanned all three floors and was built deep into the side of the volcano.

On the third floor, Aidan passed the empty offices and laboratories of the masters. It was late enough that most of the masters had retired to their rooms for the night. He stayed clear of Captain Solsti's office and her room, hoping to avoid her vibruntcy. He didn't know if she knew about his late-night journeys, but if she did, she made a point never to mention it.

Aidan approached an office door and tapped his quire processor to access the room. As the door slid open, the towering form of General Estrago sat hunched over a large metal desk.

"Ah, good evening," General Estrago said without looking up. "You're later than usual. I presume you arrived without incident."

Aidan closed the door behind him and rolled his eyes at the idea of being caught. "Nah, I was just really hungry."

General Estrago nodded while he gently tugged at his brown beard. "I see. That is probably due to the effort you exerted in the Pit today. Your body scan after the trial showed an increase in your metabolism, similar to that of a vigori prime."

With his long, massive arm, General Estrago pulled an extra chair to his desk and signaled for Aidan to take a seat. Bending over, he removed a small stack of books from a safe he kept concealed in the floor and then hefted the stack of paper books onto his desk with a thump. Stretching out his long arms, the general began cracking his back between the shoulder blades. *Pop, pop, pop, pop.*

"You did well today," the general offered as his spine continued to pop. "I tried my best to have your coterie exempt from the trials due to your small numbers, but I see my efforts were not needed."

Aidan ran his hand through his bright green hair and tried to hide the smile twitching on the ends of his gray lips. "We were lucky," he replied nonchalantly, attempting to downplay his success. "If puzzler mode hadn't kicked in, they would have destroyed us."

"Yes, well, speaking of destruction, I have a new book for you. Did you bring back the *Warrior's Mind* from our last visit?

Aidan nodded and slipped out the small, worn book from the thin compartment strapped to his chest. The compartment was housed in cortunium, making it light, strong, and invisible to the detectors throughout Mount Fegorio. It was the same material both he and General Estrago used for their secret floor compartments.

"It was an okay read," Aidan shrugged. "When I went into puzzler mode, I think I used some of the principles in the book to help me out. I could see where they were going to attack and used their own momentum and anger against them, like the book instructed."

"Very good. Then we shall fill that mind of yours with as much information as possible to assist the puzzler inside. You may not be an eidetic, but your puzzler abilities appear to have a similar eidetic gift of recall when needed."

General Estrago handed a new book to Aidan. It looked ancient with use, but the binding was strong and the green leather cover was sturdy.

Aidan read the title out loud: *"Man's Quest for Destruction: An Argument for the Prime Initiative*, by Doctor T.M. Omori." He looked back up at General Estrago. "Sounds cheerful. So the author is named after the planet where we are fighting the Splicers?"

The question amused General Estrago. "No, he was not named after the planet. The planet was named after him. He founded the first colony on Omori. Doctor Omori was quite the genius, philosopher and statesman in his time. I think you will find this tome beneficial to your education and understanding of our history."

Aidan flipped through the pages, unconvinced. "If it's so beneficial, why does the Director outlaw all of the books you give me? Why can't I just find them on my quire and read them like everything else?"

General Estrago sighed and his bushy eyebrows narrowed, causing thick creases to appear in the dark brown skin around his eyes. "That is a question for the Director," General Estrago answered. "It is one I have tried to find out, but without success. You must remember, these books and their hidden knowledge are sacred to me. They were very costly and dangerous to acquire. Need I remind you to be careful with them and keep them hidden?"

Aidan nodded. It seemed that General Estrago was always telling the prime cadets to remember this or remember that—like he worried their uneidetic minds would go blank without his constant instructions to remember.

"Don't worry," Aidan said. "I'll keep them safe, but I still don't understand why *you* keep them around if they are so dangerous. You're an eidetic—read them once and you have them memorized."

"That's a fair point," General Estrago responded, while continuing to tug at his brown beard. "The reason I collect these books is to save them for someone like you, my boy. I do not have much longer to live, and this knowledge—all knowledge—must be protected. Remember that."

General Estrago rolled his neck side-to-side, causing his thick scars to stretch and turn a lighter shade of brown as he slowly cracked away the stiffness in his neck. Aidan blanched at the long string of popping noises coming from the general. He didn't mind it when people cracked their knuckles or back, but something about hearing the neck crack just plain grossed him out.

"Begin reading the book and we will discuss your thoughts when we meet next week. I am afraid we must cut our interview short tonight. I have a research meeting to attend with Captain Solsti."

Aidan let out a whistle. "A 'research meeting,'" he teased. "I bet I know what kind of research you'll be doing with the good captain. I see the way she looks at you when you pass in the hallway. Her green eyes follow you wherever you go, which is weird and totally obvious, since she's blind. You don't have to be a puzzler to figure out she likes you."

General Estrago's cheeks burned dark brown.

"I don't know what you're talking about. She is simply my coworker and a trusted research partner. Remember, we are both doctors and scientists, in addition to our military titles. We do quite a bit of research on the side."

"Uh-huh," Aidan teased.

General Estrago harrumphed. "You are only twelve. What do you know about such things? Besides, we are primes. Do not forget that as primes enlisted in the Ethos Army, we are not allowed relationships with other primes. It blocks us from our duty, and part of that duty is procreation to sustain the prime genes. It is impossible for two primes to procreate. We must find human companions to fulfill that part of our duty."

"Whatever," Aidan said with a chuckle. "Have a good night with your 'research,' doc. I'll see you in class tomorrow."

Aidan finished securing the new book to his chest and tapped his quire to open the door.

"Sometimes I wonder why I put up with you," General Estrago groaned.

Aidan flashed a grin, exposing bright white teeth against his gray skin. "Because I'm awesome...and you're the only one who stays up this late," Aidan replied, stepping out the door. He gave the general a friendly smile and waved goodbye.

General Estrago watched as the boy confidently snuck away down the hall.

"Yes, you are awesome," he whispered to himself—a twinge of sadness resonating in his deep voice. "You remind me of your parents."

COBRAMOTH

CHAPTER 3: TRIPLE THREAT

The Splicers have gained ground on the far side of Omori. They control nearly a quarter of the planet. These creatures move with precision and in perfect unison on the battlefield. I believe they are connected telepathically, and we have found no way to disrupt their communication.

—Doctor T.M. Omori,
Man's Quest for Destruction: A Case for the Prime Initiative

Are you sure he's coming here?" Zana complained while her small blue hands fiddled with the controls of her mek suit. "It's late. I'm tired, and we've been waiting for over two hours."

"Yeah, me tired too," Wesley tapped into his commlink, his golden skin shining while he stood on a boulder at the far side of the Pit.

"Oh, I'm sorry. I thought you were senior sixteen-year primes, not newly-injected babies. Quit whining! He'll be here," Dixon hissed through the white mask covering his face. "Rumor has it he's stuck on this sim and comes every night. Now shut up and keep a lookout. That freak may have won his first trial, but he's going to pay for what he did to Kara, and I'm going to teach him what it feels like to die in the Pit."

Zana yawned, doubting she could stay awake much longer. She couldn't care less about the twelve-year vibrunt-puzzler Aidan, but Dixon had somehow hacked all three of them into simulation 299. Zana didn't know how Dixon had done it, but she couldn't pass up the chance to see Sim 299. Few primes made it past Sim 200 during their time at Mount Fegorio. She and Dixon were only on Sim 233 and they graduated in a few months.

She still didn't believe Aidan, a twelve-year cadet, had made it all the way to Sim 299. Aidan just joined the upper coteries and finished his first head-to-head trial. Most cadets his age were only on level 50 of the individual simulations. But Aidan was on Sim 299, the

legendary last level of the Pit scenarios. Such a feat
seemed impossible.

***

Aidan snuck back to his room undetected, stopping
by the commissary for one last sweet cake.

I really am hungrier than usual, he thought. Flopping
onto his bed, he cracked open the book General Estrago
loaned him, *Man's Quest for Destruction: A Case for the Prime
Initiative,* and read the first paragraph.

> *Man's natural desire is to better oneself.
> But when does this admirable attribute become a
> wedge in the growing tree of progress, destined for
> irreversible and devastating consequences? We see
> such monstrous consequences come to fruition over
> and over throughout history. When fire is not
> contained, the whole land will burn.*
>
> *The Prime Initiative is the means not only
> to contain these fires, such as the Splicers, but also
> to prevent them and protect humanity from death,
> sickness and the self-destructive horrors of our
> past that still haunt us.*

Ugh, boring, Aidan thought, tossing the book into his
secret floor compartment. He looked at his quire and
groaned. "I still have another five hours to kill until the
wake-up bell. Mr. Gloom and Doom can wait."

Aidan settled into his personal trainer seat, strapped on the headband connection and attached the adapter to his quire processor on his wrist.

"Ready for connection to the Pit," a female computerized voice read. "Entry to simulation 299 in 5-4-3-2-1."

Aidan closed his eyes and braced himself. He had never mastered a comfortable entry into the programming of the Pit. For everyone else, like Fig and Palomas, it was as easy as stepping through a doorway into another room. But for Aidan, it was akin to jumping off a skyscraper into a raging cyclone. His mind spun rapidly, catching glimpses of battleships, alien creatures and distant star systems—all intermixed with colorful, blinding flashes of light. An image appeared of a white, celestial cosmic cloud clashing with a shadowy mass of dark matter. The darkness began to overpower the light and all went black. For a split second, three glowing eyes, forming a triangle, stared at him from the darkness, and then—poof—he was in the Pit.

The spinning stopped and Aidan's vision cleared. He found himself perched atop a familiar grassy hill, overlooking a massive castle fortified by a tall wall of thick gray stones. A dense jungle and giant boulders surrounded the grassy knoll and the castle in a perfect circle. This was Simulation 299, the one individual training sim that Aidan had failed to complete.

Since receiving his own trainer seat at the age of five, Aidan had spent hours every night running sim after sim. Although he was only a twelve-year cadet, he had completed more simulations than any prime—ever.

"You are setting history," General Estrago had told him. "No one has ever made it to the current simulation you are attempting. The other masters and I are eager to see what comes next."

So was Aidan.

Unlike the other sims, where he led armies of primes against robots, raced bipods through obstacle courses and practiced underwater warfare, this was different. His assignment was to infiltrate the castle fortress and retrieve a gift hidden in the upper throne room.

One problem: the castle was laced with deadly tests he had yet to figure out. People thought Aidan did not know what it was like to die in the Pit. Truth be told, he had died hundreds of times trying to complete Sim 299. Unlike the other sims, where the pain settings were dulled to a minimum, in Sim 299 the pain settings were amplified to mimic reality, much like the pain and death one felt in the trial games against other coteries.

If I can just get my powers to meld again, he hoped, *I might actually have a chance at beating this sim.*

Aidan knew it was possible. The programming of the Pit allowed the user the ability to have their natural prime powers and any technological advances they personally created to be used in the simulation. If he had melded once, he could do it again.

"I see him," Wesley tapped into his commlink. "He go to castle. I throw rock now?"

"No!" Dixon commanded. "This is Sim 299. We are standing where no other prime has stood."

"No other prime besides Aidan," Zana corrected.

Dixon ignored the comment. "I want to see how he gets into the castle and follow him in. Once we get a look in the castle, then it's payback time for what he did to Kara."

"Whoa. Hold on, Dixon. I don't want to go inside that castle," Zana said nervously. "I only wanted to see Sim 299, not get killed in it. You go smack the kid around and then let's get out of here."

"Quit being a total wuss, Zana. You have a supersuit. You'll be fine. After we're in the castle, we can smash him, take a look around, and then jump out of the sim. Got it?"

"Fine," Zana moaned, worried that the final sim would not be so easy to navigate. "But if I get maimed or killed for no reason, you can forget about me helping you with your engineering homework."

Aidan continued toward the castle gate, oblivious to the presence of the three senior primes. He did not turn on his vibruntcy—not yet at least. He did not need it to enter the castle. All he needed were the three burning beetlants he knew he would find under the small rock near the castle moat.

The castle was surrounded by a fifty-foot-wide moat of black, foul-smelling acid. There was no bridge to

get across, and Aidan had surmised that not even a mek
suit could jump far enough to reach the gate. Even if an
agulator attempted to float across, there was one other
problem—three giant piranharays, at least twelve feet
long with huge jaws and razor-sharp teeth, would fly out
of the acid, latch onto you with their jaws, and pull you
under. Their flat, sleek bodies were covered in black
scales, which made them impossible to see under the acid,
and their powerful bodies allowed them to jump out of
the moat to incredible heights.

Aidan knew this from experience. He had
attempted using a tree branch to vault himself over, built
a raft, a bridge, and even a human slingshot to try to get
across. All had failed, with painful consequences. Either
the giant piranharays flew through the air and grabbed
him, or the acid burned through his raft while the
piranharays pulled him under.

One night, after multiple failed attempts, Aidan sat
next to the acid moat pondering his next move. An
unsuspecting burning beetlant flew onto his pant leg and
Aidan quickly flicked it into the acid lake.

WHOMP!

One of the monster piranharays flew into the air,
devoured the burning beetlant, and then froze like a wide
floating statue on top of the acid moat. After some
painful trial and error, Aidan discovered that the monster
fish went stiff for approximately one minute after eating a
burning beetlant. He also realized that if he was careful
and lined the piranharays up just right, he could cross the
moat on top of their massive floating backs.

"Did you see the size of those fish?" Zana exclaimed as they watched Aidan cross the moat from a distance.

Dixon wouldn't admit it, but the piranharays terrified him. Something was strange about this sim, and it gave him a bad feeling. "Could you see what he did to stop them from attacking?"

Zana replayed the footage she recorded from her mek suit and zoomed in. "That's weird. It looks like he tossed some burning beetlants into the moat."

"Beetlants?" Wesley questioned, clearly dumbfounded.

"Yeah, that's what I said," Zana responded. "Do you want me to spell that out for you, big guy? B-U-R-N-…"

While Zana insulted Wesley's slow-mindedness, Dixon ran at full speed towards the castle, changing his weight to a feather, and then jumped, allowing him to fly through the air. He reached the moat in time to see the hideous black fish unfreeze and begin swimming menacingly around the surface of the black moat.

Zana and Wesley caught up to Dixon, and all three stared at the swimming piranharays.

"What is that smell?" Zana complained, flipping on the air filter in her suit. "It smells like Wesley ate a bowl full of boiled eggs and spicy beans."

Dixon held his hand over his facemask to block the caustic smell of the moat from burning his nostrils, but the big lug, Wesley, didn't seem to mind.

"Wesley. Hurry and dig up some burning beetlants," Dixon commanded. "We need to get across before we lose him."

"Beetlants?" Wesley signed again, narrowing his eyes in concentration. He walked toward the acid moat. "I swim across and smash fish. It easier."

"*STOP!*" Dixon and Zana yelled in unison, but it was too late. As soon as Wesley stepped into the black moat his mouth opened in a silent screech of agony as the acid ate at his leg. A moment later, one of the huge piranharays clamped its massive jaw on his left arm. Wesley punched it in the head with devastating force, sending it flailing away in the water, but the second and third piranharays latched on before he could react. Zana flipped on her lasers and shot one of the fish in the tail, causing it to momentarily release its grip on Wesley, but it quickly recovered and both piranharays swiftly pulled Wesley under the black acid. Within seconds, the moat was still.

Zana's blue face turned three shades paler. "Okay, that looked really painful. Did you hear how he screamed?"

"Zana. He's a lug. He can't scream," Dixon said, trying to hide his own fear.

"I know that. But imagine if he could scream. That looked like a trial death, not a regular sim death. I'm out of here."

Zana tapped her quire processor to disconnect from the simulation, but nothing happened.

"What the......what's going on, Dixon? I just tried to disconnect, but nothing happened."

Dixon tried his quire with the same results.

"You've trapped us!" Zana shouted. Her normally bubbly, smiling face contorted into a look of fury as her thin eyebrows, which she meticulously plucked daily, angled down like razorblades above her eyes.

"What. Did. You. Do?!" she demanded. "What hack did you use to get us in here? I naturally assumed you coded it for a safe removal. Tuskin's fury! What if there's a flaw in your hack and we're stuck here forever? What if we die in this simulation and can never disconnect? Are we dead for real?"

"Stop it!" Dixon commanded as his mind raced through the same possibilities. "I didn't hack anything. That's just what I told you."

Dixon's white-covered head and broad shoulders drooped slightly, causing the bottom hem of his cloak to drag across the green grass next to the moat. He looked at the spot Wesley had been standing only seconds ago.

"It just appeared," he half-mumbled.

"What *just* appeared?" Zana asked icily.

Dixon took another deep breath. "The code. It just appeared. I received a message on my quire saying that I, along with two companions of my choice, could enter Sim 299 to support Aidan in completing the simulation. I saw it as my chance to get even with him for burning Kara's face in the trial. I lied about hacking the system."

"I can't believe it. You're such an idiot! Trusting an unknown hack, from a stranger, and then dragging us in with you! How are we supposed to get out of here now?"

Dixon straightened his shoulders and raised his head toward the gate. They needed to catch up to Aidan. If anyone had answers, it was him. "Let's get some burning beetlants. We need to cross this moat."

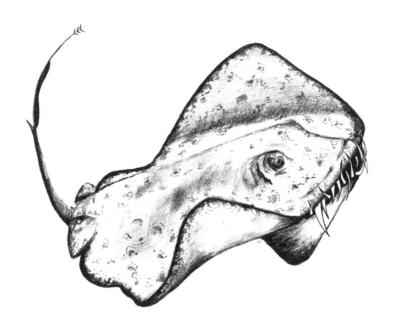

PIRANHARAY

CHAPTER 4: TESTS

The simulations in the Pit are a fascinating creation. We are still decades, if not centuries, away from uncovering the technology behind them and replicating the effects. If we can learn to control the programming, it will allow us to enhance the training and capabilities of our prime cadets.

—Doctor T.M. Omori,
Man's Quest for Destruction: A Case for the Prime Initiative

Director Tuskin sat in his chair, glued to the holovid feed of Aidan attempting simulation 299. He and the master instructors, such as General Estrago, had gained access to watch all participants in the Pit.

More like 'granted' access, the Director thought.

Much like the invitation Dixon received, the Director was provided an anonymous code two hundred years ago that allowed him and the other master instructors to record and observe all participants in the Pit.

The prime cadets were also given access to record their own simulations and replay them for study purposes. Live video feeds of the trials were made public for all of the coteries to watch in the assembly hall. But none of it was controlled by the Director or any member of the Ethos Army.

The Director bristled, knowing that this access and the programming of the Pit were both out of his control. Even his own covert Advanced Programming Unit (APU) had been unable to break past the firewalls of the Pit to gain any amount of control over the programming. Still he kept the APU working at the task in secrecy. Not even General Estrago knew about the APU's existence.

The new development of Dixon's invitation to enter simulation 299 and assist Aidan raised the Director's suspicions...and his hopes. The code Dixon received had been sent to the APU to be analyzed on a closed circuit. If there was a way to break the Pit's firewall, this code might be the key.

Still, Director Tuskin wondered who had sent the code. *Surely the creators can't still be alive*, he thought. *I was there when they died and were buried. I saw it with my own eyes.*

Yet everything in his eidetic mind pointed back to them. The triplets.

***

"Tuskin's fury!" Zana swore after reaching the gate and feeling all sleepiness vanish from her body. "That…was…freaky."

Dixon fought to control his pounding heart. One of the piranharays nearly got him, unfreezing just before he reached the gate. It jumped through the air toward him, jaws open and only a few feet away, when Dixon's foot hit the ground next to the gate. Immediately the fish fell from the air and back into the foul-smelling blackness of the acid moat.

Dixon tried to act tough, but the whole simulation was unnerving and unnatural. "We better keep moving. We don't want to lose Aidan."

Together they pushed the thick wooden gate open and stepped past the threshold of the castle.

"Are you seeing this?" Zana asked.

Dixon nodded. "I've never seen a sim do this before," he muttered.

As soon as they stepped through the gate, the sky changed from a bright noonday sun to a dark, starry night. They found themselves standing in a courtyard dimly lit by dozens of torches hanging from the inner walls.

Zana turned to look back at the gate, but it had disappeared, replaced by the stone wall of the castle grounds. "Great! We're trapped."

"Never mind that," Dixon said, pointing to the center of the courtyard. "There's Aidan."

Aidan sat cross-legged before three massive statues. He was concentrating his thoughts in an attempt to unlock puzzler mode, but the sound of voices caused him to jump. He switched on his vibruntcy and rolled to the side toward an ancient weapons rack. Grabbing a sword, he turned to the voices and stared in disbelief.

What in Omori are those two doing here? he thought.

"Uhmm, hey Aidan. What's up, man?" Zana said, waving awkwardly in her mek suit.

Aidan's muscles tightened, preparing for an attack. "Is this some kind of new test?" he asked.

Dixon floated in the air next to Zana, his white cape gently billowing in the cool breeze of the night. "Relax. Let me explain."

Aidan didn't relax.

"Listen," Dixon continued. "I received an invitation on my quire to assist you on Sim 299. The coded hack allowed me to bring two individuals with me. I brought Zana and Wesley, but Wesley was killed by those crazy piranharays. We saw how you entered and followed you in."

I hope he buys it, Dixon thought, strategically leaving out the part that he initially came here to beat and then kill Aidan himself.

Zana raised her metal mek suit arm to ask a question. "Anyways, how do we get out of here? We were kind of hoping you could tell us."

Dixon nodded. "The sim won't let us exit and we have no idea what will happen if we die here since we used a hack to get in. Dying here could kill us for real or trap us in the sim."

Aidan stared at the two senior primes, gauging their authenticity. They sounded and looked real, but it made no sense. On the other hand, in Sim 299, anything could happen.

"If you're not just a trick of the sim, tell me why you really came here. Dixon would never come to help me."

Dixon sighed. "Fine. The whole bit about receiving the invitation to this sim to help you is true. I have no idea who sent it. But I really came to ambush you after what you did to Kara in the trial. But now we need your help to get out of here."

"For the record," Zana chimed in. "I never really wanted to kill you. I just wanted to see Sim 299. And now that I have, I'm ready to leave, curl up in bed, and go back to sleep."

Aidan lowered his weapon. Against his better judgment, he believed them.

"So is there a way out?" Dixon pressed.

Aidan shook his head. "The only way out is to win or to die. You can't exit Sim 299 any other way."

"But we used a hack to get in. What does that mean for us?" Dixon asked.

Aidan hesitated. "I'm not sure…Depending on the hack, your mind could be trapped here if you die."

Thunder shook the air and a bolt of lightning ran across the sky. Dark clouds formed above the courtyard.

"Oh no, we don't have much time," Aidan paled.

"Uhmm, time for what?" Zana asked.

"Time to choose our opponent. That's how you beat the sim."

Dixon stared at Aidan confidently. "I guess we better beat our opponent."

Aidan frowned. "I've tried to beat them 93 times and failed 93 times. I'm…I'm sorry. I don't know how to beat this sim yet and the storm is a warning that we have to choose soon."

Aidan could see Zana's confused look through the mek suit control window, creases lining her blue forehead. "Uhmm, what happens if you don't pick?" Zana asked.

Aidan shrugged his shoulders. "A giant red dragleon flies into the courtyard, burns you with fire, and then eats you. It hurts a lot."

Dixon and Zana exchanged nervous glances. They anxiously searched the skyline, imagining a giant mythical dragleon swooping down for a late-night snack. They knew dragleons were not real, but anything seemed possible in this sim.

"Oh, and the same thing happens if you try to escape the courtyard and jump over the wall," Aidan continued. "He's kind of like a referee—makes you keep the rules of the sim."

Aidan walked back to the three statues in the center of the courtyard. The colossal works of art stood taller than most eidetics at ten feet high. The first statue was golden, depicting an adult lug in the simple, high-collared uniform of a prime soldier. The second was red, depicting a shirtless, muscular human in baggy red pants. The third was emerald, in the form of a massive reptilian creature.

Dixon floated close behind Aidan while Zana remained fixated on the night sky, searching for any sign of a dragleon.

"We have to choose," Aidan said, pointing to the inscription on a tablet in front of the three statues.

Choose ye now, a battle there must be.
Enemy one, enemy two, or enemy three.
Use your wit, and defeat them all.
Without an alliance, you will fall.

"What is that supposed to mean?" Dixon asked, reaching out to touch the statue of the lug.

"*NO!* Don't touch!" Aidan shouted.

Dixon quickly pulled back his hand.

"Whichever statue you touch comes to life and you have to defeat it," Aidan explained.

Dixon retreated a few steps from the statues.

"Is that what I think it is?" Zana said, pulling her attention away from the night sky to stare at the huge reptilian statue.

Aidan nodded. "Yeah. I'm pretty sure it's a Splicer. It's the toughest of the three, but they're all impossible to beat. Believe me, I've tried."

"A Splicer?" Dixon questioned in awe. "Are you sure?"

None of them had ever seen a Splicer, not even an image on the holovid or in their quires. Sure, they all knew they were training to fight the Splicers, but the Director kept any news of the war under lockdown, including what the Splicers looked like and where they came from. Supposedly, that information was on a need-to-know basis, and they didn't need to know until they were sent to Omori to fight the creatures. Rumors were all they had to describe the monsters. Rumors of invading lizard men from an alien star system.

The wind picked up as continuous thunder shook the ground and lightning shattered across the night sky.

"Crocobulls," Zana swore. "We're definitely not picking the Splicer."

"But there are three of us now," Dixon offered. "You have a senior agulator and a senior mek this time. Maybe that's what the inscription means. You need alliances to beat the sim."

Aidan knew Zana and Dixon were good fighters, some of the best at Mount Fegorio. Dixon was lean and muscular under his tight agulator uniform. Not only was he a powerful agulator, but he was agile and strong. Zana was probably the smartest mek at Mount Fegorio, besides Fig, and her mek suit was a piece of deadly mechanical art. Still, they had no idea what they were in for.

"Maybe," Aidan said. "But twenty minutes ago you were my enemies ready to kill me, too. It seems everyone wants to kill me lately."

"Hey, the enemy of my enemy," Dixon replied.

Zana walked closer to the statues. "So who do we choose?"

Aidan took a deep breath and pointed to the human.

"I last the longest against him, but be warned—he's just as deadly with that sword of his as the other two are without one."

A terrifying roar echoed overhead, above the noise of the thunder.

"It's the dragleon," Aidan said. "We have to choose now. Are you ready?"

Dixon changed his weight, falling to the ground like a boulder. Zana's mek suit hummed with power. She flipped on her laser guns and a row of rockets appeared out of her shoulders. They both nodded.

Aidan pressed his hand against the cold red stone of the human statue, his jaw set with determination.

I can't let these guys die. They shouldn't even be here. I've got to figure this out.

The statue began to shake, red light seeping from spidery cracks that formed along the stone.

"Cover your eyes," Aidan called out.

Dixon and Zana followed Aidan's command just before a burst of red light shot out from the statue. When they looked up, the statue was replaced by a giant human wielding a nine-foot broadsword.

"So you have brought friends to die with you this time, child. I shall make your deaths quick," the statue shouted triumphantly. "Who would like to taste my blade fir-"

Before he could finish speaking, Zana shot the warrior with a round of rockets from her suit. They met their target in a deafening explosion and smoke filled the courtyard.

"Now that's how you do it!" Zana shouted. "Rockets beat sword every time."

Aidan used his vibruntcy to see through the smoke. *Oh no*, he thought. "ZANA, MOVE NOW!"

Before Zana could respond, the human warrior jumped out of the smoke cloud, tackling Zana to the ground.

"You shall pay for that, devil prime," he shouted, raising his sword to impale Zana through the chest.

Dixon took a running start, lightened his weight to fly through the air, and then came crashing into the back of the warrior with a powerful kick between the shoulder blades.

The warrior flew off Zana, his sword clamoring off to the side. Dixon jumped back in the air and soared directly over the warrior, who was now lying flat on his back.

"Prepare to be crushed," Dixon taunted. He fell to the earth with all the weight he could hold inside. The warrior reached out his arms, catching Dixon by the legs and holding him in place.

"Is that all the strength you have, child?" the warrior questioned.

Dixon pushed more weight into his body than ever before. His insides shook, and he felt like he weighed more than the castle itself.

The cobblestone ground below the warrior began to crack under the pressure, but the warrior showed no signs of strain.

"You have the power of a devil Splicer within you, but I shall defeat all of the enemy Splicers and primes!" the warrior shouted. Lifting Dixon into the air, he tossed the agulator across the courtyard and into the opposite wall. Dixon slumped to the ground after impact.

Using his vibruntcy, Aidan saw Dixon's chest move up and down as he lay on the ground.

"He's still alive," Aidan shouted to Zana. "Can you keep the warrior busy? I'm going to go help Dixon."

Zana stood herself up, quickly checking her suit. "Yeah, sure thing. Keep the undefeatable psycho human warrior busy. Not a problem."

Looking to her side, Zana saw the warrior's mammoth nine-foot sword on the ground.

"Hey big guy," Zana called, hefting the sword up into the air. Thankfully her suit was powerful enough to lift it. "Are you looking for this?"

The warrior rose to his full height, towering over Zana. "You dare wield my own weapon against me?"

"Yeah. I dare," Zana said, swinging the blade at the warrior. The warrior dodged to the left, throwing a powerful kick at Zana's head in the same motion. Zana evaded the kick, swinging the blade backhanded at the warrior's feet. The warrior jumped over the sword, throwing a combo of punches that left dents in Zana's suit and pushed her backward.

Clearly outmatched, Zana retreated in a full sprint, her suit providing her a boost of unnatural speed. The warrior followed in close pursuit, giving Aidan the distraction he needed to reach Dixon unnoticed. He touched his hand to Dixon's chest and vibroscanned his body the way Captain Solsti had taught him. Using his basic knowledge from field medic class, he checked for signs of broken bones and serious injuries, but found none. Dixon was okay, but unconscious.

"Give me back my sword, so that I may slay you, demon child," the warrior bellowed.

Aidan looked up to see Zana literally cornered in the courtyard. Zana fired her remaining rockets and targeted her laser beam at the warrior.

"That tickles," the warrior responded smugly.

Still holding the sword, Zana took it by both hands and threw it over her shoulder, watching it barely clear the courtyard wall and disappear to the other side.

"Whoops. Sorry. It slipped."

The warrior screamed in outrage and grabbed Zana by both arms. He ripped the mechanical appendages free from the suit and kicked Zana to the ground. Sparks flew from where the arms had been connected. Luckily, Zana's actual arms were safe inside the control pod.

The warrior lifted his foot to stomp Zana to pieces.

"WAIT!" Aidan shouted. "It's me you want. Not her."

The warrior turned and glared. Aidan stood next to the other statues and raised his own sword in defiance. Exactly 93 times he had tried to defeat these statues, and 93 times he had failed. With Dixon's and Zana's lives on the line, he couldn't fail again

The warrior approached, eyeing the statues cautiously. "Yes, you are correct, young one. The blood of primes and Splicers runs deep in your veins. You are my true enemy."

Aidan's mind flashed in and out of puzzler mode. *Of course*, he thought. *Enemy of my enemy. Alliances.*

The warrior was only a few feet away. Aidan backed up until he stood directly between the statues of the golden lug and the emerald Splicer. "I'm not your only enemy, though. Am I?" he said, dropping his sword to the ground.

The warrior paused, his smug countenance turning dark. "After 93 painful deaths, have you finally figured it out, little one?"

Aidan reached out his hands, touching both the Splicer and the lug statues at the same time.

Only one way to find out, he thought.

The statues shook, emanating gold and green light from within. Aidan turned his back to the statues and ran to the far corner by Zana.

"Cover your eyes!" Aidan shouted to Zana. She obeyed, just as a wave of blindingly bright gold and green light shot through the air.

Aidan helped open the control hatch and gave the tiny mek a hand as she climbed out of the damaged suit. "You okay?" Aidan asked.

"Yeah, I think so. But what did you do? I was stuck on my back in the suit and couldn't see."

An ear-splitting screech echoed through the courtyard as the Splicer came to life. Aidan and Zana watched in horror as the Splicer rushed toward the human warrior with its claws extended. Its jaws opened wide to reveal rows of razor-sharp teeth in its beak-like mouth. It let out another shriek as it reached the human warrior and swung its six-inch claws at the human's face.

The human avoided the blows and sent a hard elbow to the side of the Splicer's head. Unfazed, the Splicer spun, whipping his scaly green tail around until it made contact with the back of the human's knees, sending the huge red warrior to the ground.

The human rolled to the side just in time to avoid a death-strike from the Splicer's claws. The warrior fought like a dragleon, trying to hold his own against the Splicer, but even his own incredible strength and speed was outmatched by the monster.

"I almost feel guilty for tossing his sword over the wall," Zana said, mystified by the speed and ferociousness of the battle. "He might have had a chance if he still had it."

The Splicer's claws raked across the bare chest of the human, causing him to fall to his knees and cry in pain as red blood trickled from the wound. The Splicer bent over the human, its jaws wide open as it let out another shrill shriek.

Crack!

The Splicer's battle cry was cut short. From behind, the newly awakened lug statue lifted a large castle stone out of the ground and slammed it into the Splicer's head. The Splicer backed away from the human, dazed. Seeing his opportunity, the human grabbed the largest axe he could find from the rack of weapons and chopped furiously at the Splicer's legs. Bit by bit, green blood oozed from the Splicer as the warriornicked away at its armored hide.

The lug tossed a second massive stone in the direction of the human, who ducked as it sailed overhead. The lug ran towards the human, breaking the axe with a single punch as the human swung it towards him.

As the three continued their battle royale, Aidan led Zana along the wall to where Dixon began to stir.

"Man, what happened?" Dixon asked, rubbing the back of his skull.

"You got knocked out, the human warrior ripped the arms off my supersuit, and Aidan woke up the Splicer and the lug statues," Zana answered quickly.

Dixon sat up, surveying the ongoing carnage. "You woke them all up? Why aren't they attacking us?"

Aidan grinned. "You had the answer the whole time. The enemy of my enemy is my friend. The answer was to wake all three statues and let them defeat each other."

The three giants bludgeoned, stabbed, and sliced one another—releasing red, gold and emerald light with each wound. The lug and human double-teamed the Splicer and sent him down for good, but not before the Splicer left a mortal wound to the lug with deep gouges across his neck and face. The lug stumbled for a moment and then dropped to the ground with a crash. As he fell, he threw one last stone from his hand which careened into the chest of the human. The human warrior let out a final groan, his face a mask of peace as he locked eyes with Aidan and collapsed.

"Whoa," Zana said in the silence that followed.

"What happens next?" Dixon asked in a hushed voice.

The dark clouds and nighttime sky rapidly dissolved, giving way to a stunning blue and orange sunrise. A deep roar reverberated through the courtyard as the majestic form of a dragleon circled overhead and gracefully landed before the three young primes.

The golden fur of its cat-like face glistened and its bushy brown mane bore stark contrast to the blood-red scales armoring the rest of its muscular body, wings and tail.

"Well done," the dragleon spoke in a quiet, powerful voice, revealing a row of large teeth inside its immense jaws.

Aidan thought he could see the hint of a smile on the creature's face as it spoke.

"You have passed the second test, and only one remains to complete simulation 299."

Zana's eyes went wide with horror. "You mean we're not done yet?"

The dragleon half-snarled and half-laughed.

"Yes and no. You've met your challenge well this day and you are now allowed to return home, but you must return in three weeks to complete your quest. All three of you must return, or there will be grave consequences."

Aidan, Dixon and Zana eyed one another. A simulation couldn't threaten them in the real world, could it?

"What do you mean?" Aidan asked. "What consequences?"

The dragleon bared his teeth and produced a low guttural growl. "If you must know to obey, I will tell you. If all three of you do not return, you will never be allowed to enter the Pit again, and your abilities to access any quire processor will be revoked permanently."

"He can't do that, can he?" Dixon whispered to Aidan. Without their quires, they couldn't do anything. They used their quires to print food, play games, study for class, enter sims, and drive bipods.

"Yes, I can," bellowed the dragleon. "My creators have granted me the power to do so. They were the original creators of the Pit and the quires. They have also instructed me that you be sworn to secrecy. You must not share how you defeated the statues or anything else regarding your experience in this simulation going forward. This includes your own coteries and even the masters. If you break this rule, the same consequences will apply."

The dragleon turned its gaze towards Zana. Its eyes locked on her, as if peering into her thoughts.

"Lastly, young Zana. You need not fear death in the Pit. Death is not permanent here, but be warned, it will be painful. Remember that pain is a teacher. Love is life. You may now retire, for it is morning in your realm. Return in exactly three weeks' time, or face the consequences."

Aidan took a step towards the dragleon, his fears of the beast swept aside by an innate connection he felt with the creature. The dragleon sat on his haunches, unmoving as Aidan approached. Aidan's mind raced with questions, but only one formed on his lips, and he knew it was the one he had to ask.

"Do you have a name?"

The dragleon bowed his head toward Aidan. "I am the protector of the law, caretaker of this realm and keeper of secrets. I am Sentinel."

DRAGLEON

CHAPTER 5: SECRETS

The coterie system was an important development of the Prime Initiative. In the beginning, when worthy newborn candidates were taken for treatment, they were separated and raised according to their prime abilities. We soon found that this process hindered their growth and potential, causing extreme divisions among them.

The coterie system divided the primes by age, regardless of their abilities, with twelve primes in each coterie. This provided them with a deeper connection and understanding of one another's abilities, creating more cohesion on the war front after they graduated from their respective facilities. The coterie system also had the surprising effect of creating pseudo familial bonds. On their own, coterie members began calling each other brother and sister.

—Doctor T.M. Omori,
Man's Quest for Destruction: A Case for the Prime Initiative

STRAGO!" the Director yelled from the holovid. "ESTRAGO. I NEED YOU NOW!" The large eidetic flinched, surprised to hear Director Tuskin's voice shouting at him while he shaved in front of the mirror in his room. The flinch caused him to nick one of the scars on his neck just below his neatly trimmed beard. Dark brown blood pooled around the tiny cut and began to roll down his collar.

"ESTRAGO! WHERE ARE YOU?!"

Quickly rinsing off his face, General Estrago held a white towel to the cut on his neck to stanch the bleeding. He entered his main living quarters to find an image of Director Tuskin's face floating on the holovid.

"Yes, Director," he responded with a bow of the head.

"Go to Aidan's room immediately! Make sure he is unhurt. Hurry and report to me right away!"

Before General Estrago could respond with follow-up questions, the Director's image disappeared.

What's happened? Estrago thought, as worry-filled creases pushed along his forehead. He hastily dressed himself and sped towards Aidan's room with the elongated stride of a ten-foot-tall eidetic.

Director Tuskin switched off the holovid, his skin flashing gold as he slammed his fist into his desk, breaking it in two.

"They dare shut me out of the simulation. I swear, if that boy is hurt…" he growled. His eidetic mind recalled the last image he saw of Aidan as the boy raised a sword in defiance toward the human warrior. Then all went blank. A single sentence appeared in block letters across the empty holovid.

This is not your secret.

***

"Aidan! Aidan! Wake up, bro!" Fig yelled into Aidan's face. Fig stood on a chair next to Aidan, his concern growing. He had been trying to wake up Aidan for the last ten minutes, until he eventually called Palomas for help.

Palomas shook Aidan. When he did not respond, she shook his limp body harder.

"Whoa, Palomas. Relax!" Fig said, putting his tiny hand on her arm. "You're going to hurt him."

Palomas let go, suddenly realizing what she was doing.

"Sorry," she signed with shaky hands. "He's not waking up. We need to get help. Now!"

Aidan's door slid open, causing Palomas and Fig to jump. The towering figure of General Estrago entered the room and they quickly rose to attention, offering a crisp salute.

"What's going on? Is Aidan okay?" General Estrago asked, rushing to Aidan's side in one long stride.

Aidan sat peacefully in his trainer's seat, unresponsive to the commotion around him.

"We don't know, sir," Fig replied. "I came into his room to go with him to breakfast and found him like this." Fig waved his hand at Aidan's comatose body.

"He's still breathing, but he won't move," Palomas added. "Can you help him?"

General Estrago tapped the quire processor attached to his wrist and scanned Aidan's body. His training as a doctor took over as he read the scan.

"His vitals are fine. Did you try to disconnect him from the seat?"

Palomas and Fig shook their heads.

"Good. We don't know what disconnecting him will do. To my eidetic knowledge, this has never happened before with a sim. Disconnecting him may cause brain damage or death. We must err on the side of caution."

General Estrago attempted to sync his quire to Aidan's, which was connected to the trainer seat, but it would not sync. A message appeared on his quire.

This is not your secret.

"This is odd," General Estrago muttered.

"What's odd? What is it, sir?" Fig asked. The three-foot tall blue mek jumped on a nearby chair to stand a little taller as he spoke to General Estrago.

General Estrago shook his head and tugged at his beard. "I don't know. I can't access his system at all. He seems to be trapped in a simulation. My guess is that it's Sim 299."

General Estrago turned to Fig and Palomas, narrowing his eyes. "I need both of you to leave right now. I must call for support and make a report."

Palomas stood firm. "We're not going anywhere…sir" she signed. Her timid facial expression showed her personal uneasiness at disobeying a direct order from her commanding officer.

General Estrago sighed. His enlarged heart was racing from his rush to reach Aidan. He would need to take his medication soon and the stress of Aidan's condition was not helping his heart.

"While I admire your sense of loyalty," General Estrago said between heavy breaths, "I must speak with Director Tuskin in person. You *cannot* stay. Do you understand?"

Fig's and Palomas' eyes went wide. No one "saw" the Director. He was always hidden from view. Some people wondered if he even existed anymore. Rumor was those who saw the Director did not live to tell the tale.

"Please," General Estrago asked, more forcefully this time. "Go now. I will watch over him."

Reluctantly, Fig and Palomas left the room and headed to the commissary.

"Do you think he will be alright?" Palomas signed.

Fig shrugged. "I think so. I'm more worried about why the Director cares about it."

Palomas nodded. Anything involving the Director was sure to be dangerous. When the Director was involved, people disappeared.

They walked through the commissary doors, and Fig's stomach growled like a kangadog as the smells of warm breakfast wafted through the air.

"No use worrying about it on an empty stomach," Fig said, dashing in line to print his breakfast and load up his plate.

Palomas frowned at Fig, shaking her head slightly. Looking around the room, she paused. Something was off. All of the tables were full with their coteries, except one. She frowned. *Where are the sixteen-year seniors?*

Curious, Palomas walked back into the main hallway and circled down the central ring of the second level in the direction of the senior dorms. As other cadets passed her, they took a few steps to the side to clear a path. Although she was only twelve, Palomas had a bit of a reputation as one of the toughest lugs in the complex. Even among the older coteries, Palomas was respected.

She reached the senior girls dorm and pressed the door buzzer. No one answered. She knocked loudly. Still no answer. She thought about knocking really hard and breaking down the door, but knew that would only get her in trouble. She looked across the hallway and tried the boys door with a loud knock. After a few seconds, it slid open and one of the senior cadets, a tall, skinny eidetic girl named Ameera, opened the door.

"What do *you* want?" Ameera sneered.

Palomas heard crying in the background and pushed her way into the room. The senior dorms were much larger than her room, with rows of beds, multiple washrooms and multiple trainers seats, which made sense since they were one of the largest coteries at the complex with five boys and five girls still alive from their original twelve.

Palomas found the seniors gathered around two trainer seats. One held Dixon, the senior coterie captain, and the other held Zana. Kara stood next to the unconscious form of Dixon, whimpering over him while she held his hand and stroked his head. "We have to help him," she cried.

On the floor, with his knees tucked in close, sat Wesley, a senior lug. Tears streamed down his face. "It hurt bad," he signed repeatedly. "I still feel it."

Palomas tried to take stock of the situation. Seeing Wesley, someone she admired for his toughness, sitting like a scared child on the floor was one thing. But seeing Kara, a fifteen-year prime, holding Dixon's hand and stroking his head was another.

"I'm going to disconnect him from the chair," Kara announced. None of the seniors argued as she reached to remove the headband connection. Palomas rushed forward and pushed Kara away.

"What do you think *you're* doing?" Kara shouted.

"Stop," Palomas signed. "Disconnecting him could kill him."

"Why you little monster. How dare you! Get away from him," Kara yelled, swinging her fist at Palomas with the power of a sledgehammer. Palomas caught Kara's fist in her open hand, stopping the blow midair, and began to slowly squeeze. Kara's hand bones started cracking in Palomas' grip.

Palomas shook her head and Kara yielded, pulling back to nurse her hand.

"Do not disconnect them," Palomas signed. "The same thing is happening to Aidan. General Estrago is looking at him right now and is in direct contact with Director Tuskin about it."

There was an audible gasp at the mention of the Director.

"I think there is a glitch in the simulation system and they are trapped inside," she continued. "General Estrago said disconnecting them could kill them."

Palomas could not see Kara's face behind the white mask, but she imagined it twisted in anger. "This is that freak Aidan's fault. I know it is," she hissed, stomping out of the room.

Palomas looked at the remaining seniors, who stared at her with a mixture of loathing and deference. "Wesley," she signed to the cowering lug. "What happened?"

"He won't answer," Ameera said. "All we've gotten out of him is that they went where they should not have gone. Then something about acid and piranharays. He keeps repeating himself about the pain."

"So he was in the sim with the rest of them?"

"We think so, but who knows?"

This new information only confused Palomas more.

"Stay with them and don't let anyone try to disconnect them manually. I will let General Estrago know they are trapped as well."

The seniors nodded, including Ameera, and Palomas left the room.

Fig caught a glimpse of Palomas in the hallway through the commissary window. "Where did you run off to?" he asked, running out of the commissary to catch up to her.

Palomas explained the situation with the seniors as they hurried to Aidan's room. Palomas buzzed Aidan's door, but no one answered. "Back up," she signed. "I'm going to rip the doors open."

"Whoa, sis. Relax with those super muscles of yours," Fig said, pulling out a tiny cylinder device, about the size of a finger, from his pocket.

Palomas was not surprised to see the device. Fig was always tinkering and building new gadgets. She eyed this one suspiciously, wondering what it did.

"Let's take a listen before you start breaking down doors. The Director might be in there and I don't want to die today."

He pulled on the tube, elongating it, and revealed a suction cup on one end and two wireless earpieces on the other. "I call them 'vibrunt ears,'" he whispered. "They're definitely not as cool as being a vibrunt, but you can hear through most walls and listen to people up to 100 feet away. I tested them the other night and they worked great…by the way, you snore in your sleep."

Palomas let out a breathy gasp. "I do not snore!" she signed.

Fig ignored her and connected the miniscule suction cup to the wall. "C'mon. Let's go to my room," he whispered. "I don't want to get caught standing outside his door."

Safely inside Fig's room, Fig passed one of the earpieces to Palomas. She took it, hesitated for just a moment, and put it in her ear. She knew they were breaking the first rule of mek technology—never use tech made by another mek's hands. Still, their coterie had been breaking this rule for years and nothing bad had happened—yet. But if anyone found out, she knew there would be serious consequences.

Fig placed the other earpiece in his ear and turned on the gadget. They were met with an unfamiliar voice.

"Have his coterie companions left?" the unfamiliar voice asked.

"Yes," General Estrago answered. "They have retired to Cadet Figirol's room."

The unfamiliar voice grunted his approval. "Are you sure he is okay?" he asked.

"His vitals are fine, but I'm afraid we will have to wait and see if he can disconnect on his own," General Estrago answered.

"You had better go check on the senior primes Dixon and Zana. They were in the simulation with Aidan when my connection was blocked."

Fig and Palomas tried to hide their shock, knowing they were being recorded by hidden cameras in the room. The unfamiliar voice had to be Director Tuskin.

"But Director, that should not even be possible. What were those two seniors doing in there? Aidan was on his private trainer seat. Coteries can't intermix in simulations except during trials when using the trainer seats in the assembly hall."

"That's the question of the hour," the Director responded. "Keep me posted on any updates."

The conversation went silent. Fig and Palomas waited for more, but nothing came. There was a knock at their door and Fig's face flushed with fear.

"Open it," Palomas signed.

"What if it's the Director here to kill us?" he signed back to Palomas.

Palomas rolled her eyes. "Fine. I'll open it."

Palomas walked to the door and pressed the button to unlock it. The door slid open to expose the massive form of General Estrago.

Fig and Palomas came to attention and saluted.

General Estrago smiled sympathetically and returned the salute. "You may come back to his room now. You are both excused from classes today. I need you to keep an eye on him until I return."

Palomas and Fig traded glances and nodded.

"Yes, sir," Fig said. "At least one good thing is coming out of this. I get to miss Lieutenant Henderson's class on mek inventions. That guy is the biggest jer-"

Fig stopped, realizing he was sharing his thoughts out loud again.

General Estrago raised an eyebrow. "Is there a problem with Lieutenant Henderson's instruction?" he asked gruffly.

Besides the fact that he's a psycho, grumpy old human who hates primes, gives loads of classwork, and always looks angrier than a crocobull? Fig thought. But Fig kept silent this time and shook his head in the negative.

"Very good. I will inform Lieutenant Henderson of your situation, and I'm sure he will be more than happy to provide you makeup classwork."

Fig's head and shoulders slumped at the prospect of *makeup work* from Lieutenant Henderson. He knew the lieutenant would not be happy about his absence and he prepared himself for not only makeup work, but extra work the lieutenant would surely add out of spite.

"General, sir," Palomas signed. "Is Aidan going to be alright?"

General Estrago bit his lip and pulled at his thick beard with his right hand. "Aidan is very resourceful. I'm sure he will be fine. Call me via your quires if there is any change and I will come back immediately. Understood?"

"Yes, sir!" Palomas and Fig replied resolutely and gave a sharp salute.

"Very good. I must go attend to a few other students and I will be back later today."

General Estrago returned Palomas' and Fig's salutes, then left the room.

"I'll tell you whose fault this is," Fig whispered, once General Estrago was out of earshot. "Those two senior punks did this to Aidan, and it's their fault I'm going to get stuck with extra work from Lieutenant Henderson. I bet this was all Zana's plan. She's always trying to get me in trouble with Henderson."

Palomas slapped Fig across the back of the head and rolled her eyes. "You're an idiot," she signed. "Zana is stuck in a coma of her own. I doubt she planned this just to get revenge on you. Plus, Aidan is still passed out and you're worried about Lieutenant Henderson?"

Fig shook his head. "You have no idea. Just wait until you and Aidan take your first class with him this week. Then you'll understand. The guy is totally crazy."

"You know what I don't get," Palomas signed as they entered Aidan's room. "How did Dixon, Zana and Wesley hack into Sim 299?"

"I know. Those three are not *that* smart. Especially Wesley. That kid's slower than a snailmunk. Someone had to have helped them."

Palomas nodded and took a seat next to Aidan, held his hand and gently stroked it the same way she had seen Kara console Dixon.

Aidan's fingers twitched at her touch. Then his hand grabbed hers, his eyes burst open, and he gasped for air.

"Aidan. Man, are you okay?" Fig asked, standing on his chair so Aidan could see him.

Aidan removed the headband and disconnected his quire. "Yeah. I think so." He stood up from the trainer seat and rubbed his head. "What are you guys doing here?"

They told Aidan about everything that had happened since they found him unconscious in the trainer seat that morning. He quickly relayed his time in Sim 299 with Dixon and Zana, stopping the story just before he awakened the lug and Splicer statues.

"Then what happened?" Palomas asked.

Aidan shook his head. "I…I can't tell you guys."

"What do you mean you can't tell us?" Palomas demanded. "Do Dixon and Zana know what happened next?"

Aidan nodded. "It's something we can't share with anyone. We were sworn to secrecy. I'm sorry."

Fig grimaced. "You mean you can talk to those two jerks about it, but not us? We share everything!"

"I'm sorry," Aidan repeated. "It's the way it has to be."

SPIDERGOOSE

CHAPTER 6: MEK TECH

For hundreds of years, the inventions of meks have revolutionized Ethos and the other planets: the bipod hover vehicles, printable food and clothing, all-terrain mek suits, and much more. But it comes with the limitations of the mek defect. Perhaps one day those limitations will be fixed. Perhaps then, meks can successfully repair and retrofit our original starships used in the pilgrimage to this system. It could provide us a means of escape.

—Doctor T.M. Omori,
Man's Quest for Destruction: A Case for the Prime Initiative

Y ou're telling me three eight-year-old kids, identical triplets, created all of the programming for the Pit?" Aidan asked.

"Essentially, yes," General Estrago answered, tugging at his neatly trimmed beard.

"So if I understand correctly, you and the other masters, even the Director, don't really know how the simulations work, and you have no idea what's after Sim 299."

General Estrago raised his bushy eyebrows and pursed his lips. "Well, if you and the other two cadets would be more forthcoming about what happened in the simulation, I may be able to use the information to gather more answers."

Aidan shook his head adamantly. "We can't. Like I explained before, we have to keep it secret."

General Estrago frowned. "Indeed." He fought to stifle a yawn and looked at the time on his quire processor. The late-night hour had turned to early morning, and fatigue was setting in.

"On another note, have you been reading the material I last lent you? The one by Doctor T.M. Omori?"

Aidan remembered the book and wrinkled his nose as if smelling a large pile of bearcat dung. "The destruction book? It was drier than the Plains of Cisco in Sim 63. I tried the first chapter and nearly fell asleep."

"But you don't sleep," General Estrago pointed out.

"My point exactly. It's called a joke, General. You're supposed to laugh."

General Estrago opted to release a deep sigh rather than laugh. He laid his meaty hand on Aidan's shoulder and it nearly wrapped around the top quarter of the boy's body, reminding Aidan how big the general truly was.

"Aidan, I must insist that you continue reading. As I've taught before, 'studying our history is the key to our future.' The warfare history lessons I give you and the other cadets in the classroom are the watered down versions of the truth. That's what I am forced to teach you. But it is books like this one and our late-night conversations where you will learn about our true past. Do you understand? Will you continue your study of the book?"

Aidan's head waffled back and forth until finally he nodded in consent.

General Estrago grunted his approval. "Now, unlike you, I begin to grow weary and must rest."

"What, no midnight rendezvous with Captain Solsti?"

General Estrago's eyes went wide and he pursed his lips preparing to offer a rebuttal.

Aidan waved his hands back and forth. "Sorry. Just another joke. Laughter, remember. But I do have another question. A serious one this time. It has to do with my entries into the simulations. Every time I enter the Pit, I see the same images for a split second."

Aidan paused, closing his eyes to concentrate on the image in his mind.

"Go on," General Estrago encouraged. "What do you see?"

"I see a bright white cosmic cloud clashing with a mass of dark matter. The darkness starts to overpower the light and then everything goes black. From the darkness, three white eyes, in a triangle, stare at me. They don't look angry or sad. They look almost happy to see me. Does that mean something?"

General Estrago frowned. "I don't know," he answered honestly, storing the information away in the vaults of his eidetic mind.

***

"Who can tell me the first rule of mek engineering?" Lieutenant Henderson barked in a sharp voice.

Lieutenant Henderson paced back and forth across the front of the classroom. His small five-foot frame was dwarfed by an eidetic boy sitting on the front row, causing him to momentarily disappear from view each time he passed in front of the eidetic.

"Come now, you should have learned this rule by your fourth year as primes," he bellowed. Red splotches developed on the pinkish skin of his cheeks. Aidan found the human coloring fascinating, and it made him happy to see someone else besides himself with multiple colors to their body.

"We talked about this last week, and now it's time to review. Does anyone care to share the answer? Anyone!"

Lieutenant Henderson paused, staring across heads of the primes sitting silent in the four rows of stadium seats in the room. His jaw clenched, causing tight lines to form around his blue eyes. Fig found the man's blue eyes, pink skin, gray hair and gray goatee rather distracting and annoying.

The guy's like a rainbow of color, Fig thought. *A very angry and very old rainbow.*

As Henderson droned on, Fig zoned out, remembering his long morning earlier that day in Mek Inventions class, which was also taught by Lieutenant Henderson. Mek Inventions was a mek-only class, and Henderson, the only human master instructor at Mount Fegorio, was the instructor.

In the class, Lieutenant Henderson had given each mek a box of random parts.

"You have three hours to build a weapon to defend yourself using only these spare parts," he barked at them. "So get your lazy rears in gear and start working!"

At first, Fig loved the project. He lost himself in the joys of building a bo staff that shot short-burst electrical charges out the tips at either end. He incorporated an electromagnetic pulse into the ends of the staff that he could use as a weak forcefield to deflect small metal projectiles or disrupt enemy electronics within a few feet away. He could also use the electromagnets to attract metal objects from nearby, such as weapons out of the hands of enemies. All in all, Fig was proud of his electrostaff creation.

Fig, you've outdone yourself again, he thought.

"What is that you have, Cadet Figirol?" Lieutenant Henderson snapped at Fig.

Fig bristled at being called Figirol. He hated his proper name. Fig suited him much better.

"It's an electrostaff, sir," Fig replied, proudly going into detail about how the staff worked.

Lieutenant Henderson shook his head and sneered. "You meks are all the same. Always stealing tech from one another. Not an original idea in your bones."

Fig looked aghast at the accusation. He had just spent three hours making an awesome piece of tech that was completely original, since he had come up with it on the spot.

"What do you mean unoriginal?! You couldn't come up with an invention like this if you had three years, let alone three hours!" Fig's eyes went wide as he realized he had spoken his thoughts out loud again.

Lieutenant Henderson's face turned crimson. "Why, you little—that's two hours extra coursework for your insubordinate tone, two more hours for not saying *sir* when talking to an officer, and two more hours for lying. You stole this idea from cadet Zana, and don't try to deny it!"

Lieutenant Henderson pointed a bony finger toward Zana, who stood in the opposite corner of the room a few rows behind Fig. She was holding what looked to be a similar bo staff to the one in his own hands, but she was much too far away for either of them to have copied designs off one another.

"She has the exact same specs and accessories on her staff as you. Clearly you see fit to copy the work of older and smarter meks, now that you're no longer in the low-level coterie division."

"Excuse me!" Fig retorted, jumping onto his chair to reach Lieutenant Henderson's eye level. "I didn't copy off her, *sir!* I can barely see her from here. If anyone copied someone, she copied me!"

"Cadet Figirol," Fig heard a voice call from the back of his mind.

"Cadet Figirol, will you wake up!" Lieutenant Henderson shouted at the top of his lungs.

Fig felt a hard elbow from Palomas, causing him to jump in his seat. His eyes shot open and a dreaded realization dawned on him. He had dozed off in class.

"You've just earned yourself two more hours of coursework for sleeping in my class, Cadet Figirol. Your insubordination seems to have no end today. Daydreaming in my class will keep you repeating it for many years. Isn't that right, Cadet Wesley?"

The senior lug raised his head slightly at the sound of his name, but his lost eyes and hollow expression betrayed his lack of comprehension. Though Wesley had never been particularly bright, since his death in Sim 299, his mind appeared almost numb.

"Precisely," continued Lieutenant Henderson. "Cadet Figirol, now that you've returned to us from your childish nap, you can answer the question, if you please."

Fig stared blankly. He wasn't sure how long he had been asleep and he had no idea what question Lieutenant Henderson was demanding an answer for. Seeing his brother in trouble, Aidan raised his hand and began speaking.

"The first rule of mek engineering is to never use technology made by mek hands. It must be assembled by yourself or a human at all times."

Lieutenant Henderson's blue eyes zeroed in on Aidan, who was seated on Fig's right side.

The lieutenant gave a curt shake of his head. "Tsk. Tsk. Tsk. I don't care that you are a supposed puzzler genius, Cadet Aidan, but you would do well not to speak out of turn and to address me as *sir*. You just received an additional two hours of coursework for yourself."

Aidan's jaw dropped. He had never received extra coursework or been reprimanded by a master instructor before, especially after giving the correct answer to a question.

Lieutenant Henderson huffed as he stared at Aidan. "Well then, puzzler Aidan. Since you're *so* much smarter than the rest of us, perhaps you can remind the class as to why this first rule of mek engineering is in place."

Aidan exhaled slowly, giving Fig a quick glance. He knew Fig hated the reasoning behind this rule, and Aidan could already see Fig clenching his jaw in anger. Aidan knew if he answered this question in front of the class, it was going to cause problems.

"The reason behind this rule," Aidan responded hesitantly, "is the issue of the mek defect. Dwarfism is not the only defect seen in meks. All meks inherently sabotage their own creations so only they can use their own tech."

Fig began to squirm in his seat, his fists clenched on the desk in front of him.

"But it's not their fault," hurried Aidan. "They don't do it on purpose. It happens subconsciously and they're not even aware of it. If you asked a mek how they sabotaged their tech, they would have no idea. They couldn't tell you if they honestly wanted to."

Aidan looked to see if his answer had placated Fig, but Fig had not relaxed. His lip curled in disgust as he stared at Lieutenant Henderson.

Lieutenant Henderson gave a single, curt nod to Aidan. "Your answer is acceptable, although your defense of mek sabotage is only partially true. There are many records of meks knowingly and willingly sabotaging their tech and designs. But even when they do it subconsciously, as you presume, it's led to some of the worst disasters in the Ethos Army. May I remind all of you about the early tragedies of this war, such as the loss of the battleship Orion and the explosion of the Mount Scolus complex nearly two hundred years ago. Over one thousand primes and human soldiers were needlessly lost in those incidents, all due to using mek technology built by meks and *sabotaged* by meks."

Lieutenant Henderson paused for effect, letting his tirade sink into the students' minds.

"That is why the human engineering corps is needed," he said proudly, raising his head slightly in the air. "The human engineering corps reverse engineers all mek tech, redesigns it *properly*, and builds it so it can be *safely* used in the war effort."

Fig had had enough. He slammed his fists into the table and stood on his chair. "And that's probably why we're losing the war!" he shouted across the room.

"Excuse me. Did you say something, Cadet Figirol? My, you are a glutton for punishment."

Aidan laid a gentle hand on Fig's shoulder and attempted to pull him back to his seat, but Fig shook it off. Once he got angry, all his fear and inhibition vanished, as Aidan and Palomas knew all too well.

"I said, that's why we're probably losing the war. It takes the humans thirty years to reverse engineer one of our designs that we could make in three weeks. You guys do an okay job, but it takes you forever. If you would just let us meks consult with you when you reverse engineer and work with you on the tech, we could speed the process up ten times."

Lieutenant Henderson's eyes narrowed, and he crossed his arms as he stood behind the metal pulpit at the front of the room. "That will be quite enough. I will not have you condescend down to me. You think you're better because you are a prime?"

"No," Fig said, sitting down. "I'm just a better engineer than you will ever be, and I'm only twelve. Oh, and by the way, I constantly share my tech with my coterie. As long as I use it with them at the same time we never have any problems. Just the other day I tested out new tech with Palomas. We both put it in our ears and no one died. It worked perfectly."

Fig caught his breath, realizing he had spoken his private thoughts out loud once again.

Aidan groaned, and Palomas stared at Fig in disbelief. They were busted.

Audible gasps came from the other students, and the class went abuzz with chatter. Lieutenant Henderson's tight red lips spread into a wide grin. He pushed a few buttons on his podium, and a metal restraint, made of cortunium, whipped out from Aidan's, Palomas' and Fig's chairs. It wrapped around each of their midsections, pinning their arms to the side while another band came across their legs, securing them fast to their seats.

The gossiping class went silent. Lieutenant Henderson had used the emergency security bands, built to restrain primes dangerously misusing their powers.

"For your blatant disregard for the rules of technology, I penalize you to the full extent of the Ethos Army regulation 36.3 section A. You each will receive five electrical lashings!"

The class was stunned. Electrical lashings were a rarity. The last time someone received lashings was when a fight broke out between two agulators that left the commissary in ruins. Even then, they had only received one lashing each.

Fig and Palomas squirmed, but the cortunium bands only tightened. Palomas tried to break the restraints, but with her arms pinned so tightly she had no leverage to move.

Aidan sat calmly and stared at Lieutenant Henderson. "You know this is wrong. The punishment is too severe."

"Is it?" Lieutenant Henderson questioned, fire in his eyes. "This rule is the most important rule in the Ethos Army. By breaking this rule, you have put all the lives of those residing in Mount Fegorio in danger! You three will learn to keep this rule, so help me!"

He pushed another button on his podium. Aidan clenched his teeth as the restraints sent a powerful electrical current pulsing through his body. Fig screamed while Palomas contorted her face as they endured the same pain. After a few seconds the electric current ceased.

"One," Lieutenant Henderson called out and pressed the button again.

The painful shock of electricity coursed through their veins a second time, causing the hair on their heads to stand straight up in the air.

"That's two," Lieutenant Henderson taunted, holding up two fingers before bringing them down on the button again. A third shock sizzled through their bodies. Aidan had felt the pains of multiple injuries and deaths in Sim 299, but the lashings were different. Every nerve in his body screamed as if on fire, but unlike the Pit where the sweet peace of death would end the pain, here it continued. The lashings were programmed to inflict the highest amount of pain possible without letting the victim pass out or die. It was the ultimate tool of torture.

The third shock ended, and Aidan's head slumped forward. A small voice whispered in the back of his mind.

Pain is a teacher. Love is life.

"How is this teaching me anything?" Aidan moaned out loud.

"Three," Lieutenant Henderson announced, a gleeful smile stretched across his face. "You primes think you're so high and mighty. You think you're better than us humans. Let me tell you, you're not! You were once human, just like me, and just like my wife and children were. Without us humans, there would be no prime army and no technology for you to use. You enjoy the fruit of our slave labor with no respect for the work we do!"

The class stared in stunned silence as Lieutenant Henderson went from his normal crazy to completely unhinged.

"You destroyed my life after I gave *EVERYTHING* to this war! Let this be a lesson to you. You need to be humbled!"

Lieutenant Henderson raised his finger ceremoniously to press the button again, but before he could inflict another lashing, a golden form rammed into the podium like a crocobull at full speed. It was Wesley, the senior lug. The podium slammed into the wall, and Lieutenant Henderson was thrown to the side. Drops of red blood dripped from a small cut in his lip and splashed onto his neatly pressed tan uniform, staining it red. Lieutenant Henderson rubbed the back of his head, slightly dazed, and then patted his bleeding lip with his sleeve.

With the podium demolished, the restraints pinning Aidan, Fig, and Palomas to their seats retracted back into their chairs.

"How dare you!" Lieutenant Henderson shouted, still dabbing at his bloodied lip. "You've just sealed your failure in this class for the fourth time, Cadet Wesley! You will never pass this class! Never! I will see you imprisoned and lashed ten times daily for your attack. Do you understand me?!"

Wesley grabbed Lieutenant Henderson by the front of his uniform, and with one hand he lifted him into the air. Lieutenant Henderson's eyes bulged, and his face flushed red as he spit and sputtered a mixture of saliva and blood in complete outrage. With his remaining hand, Wesley slowly signed, "You not nice. You mean. You hurt kids. I hurt you."

Wesley reared back his thick golden arm, ready to level a deadly blow to Lieutenant Henderson's skull. The lieutenant's face drained ashen white. He shook his head emphatically, and beads of sweat began to roll down his face to the high collar of his tan-colored uniform.

"No, no, please stop," he whimpered.

Everyone knew, including Lieutenant Henderson, that one punch from Wesley would be lights out, permanently. It would also mean Wesley's swift execution for assaulting a superior officer and master instructor.

"Stop, Wesley," Aidan said forcefully. Wesley turned and watched Aidan walking to the front of the class. Aidan put his hand on Wesley's raised arm and gently pulled it down.

"It's okay. I think Lieutenant Henderson has learned his lesson. He will try to be nicer from now on. Won't you, sir?"

Lieutenant Henderson nodded rapidly.

Aidan turned to the class. "And we should all show more appreciation for our instructor. He is a master, and a human and deserves our respect," Aidan offered sincerely.

Lieutenant Henderson tilted his head, his eyebrows drawing together in confusion. It was an odd sight to see, with his feet still dangling three feet in the air under Wesley's grasp.

"Please put him down, Wesley," Aidan asked, calmly. "It will be okay."

Aidan was somewhat surprised when the senior actually obeyed him. Wesley dropped the lieutenant to the ground, who landed sharply on his rear end with a thud. Aidan bent down low, blocking the class from Lieutenant Henderson's view.

"Someone once told me that pain is a teacher, and love is life," he whispered to Lieutenant Henderson. "I've just saved your life. But if you ever attack me, my coterie, or another cadet again, I promise you will know pain."

Lieutenant Henderson swallowed. "I…I understand."

HIPPOPHANT

CHAPTER 7: VIBRUNT

Carrying the weight of this war is a lonely role. I am not blind to the pain, suffering and loss it incurs, but I must blind my feelings like a vibrunt's eyes, and open my thoughts to the whole picture if we are to succeed. With every war, sacrifices must be made.

—Doctor T.M. Omori,
Man's Quest for Destruction: A Case for the Prime Initiative

Kara, you have to understand. It was my fault, not Aidan's," Dixon pleaded as he and Kara floated thirty feet in the air in the corner of the empty assembly hall.

A vent duct ran along one end of the wall, leaving a narrow space with just enough room for them to meet without prying eyes. The assembly hall was well shielded from UV rays, since it was buried deep into the side of the volcano, and they felt safe to take off their masks here. This little corner of the assembly hall was their spot. It was the first place they had kissed.

"Don't get mad at the kid," Dixon continued. "I used a code to hack into Sim 299 with Zana and Wesley, and I entered the sim to get revenge against him for what he did to you in the trial...but then we got stuck. Aidan saved our lives."

"And did you get revenge?" Kara sneered, ignoring the whole part about Aidan saving Dixon's life. "It seems like you two are new best friends. You spend more time with him than you do with me—always off to your little secret meetings with him and Zana. What, you don't think I notice? Do you have any idea what others are saying about you?"

Dixon shrugged. "So what? If they have something to say, they can say it to my face. Aidan's actually a pretty cool kid once you get to know him. Plus, we have to get together so we can prepare for our next jump into Sim 299. Who cares what others think? They can get over it."

Kara whipped back her white hair and threw up her hands. "*Who* cares what others think? I CARE! My friends think you went crazy in the sim just like Wesley, and I'm beginning to believe them. And I still don't approve of you going back into that sim, especially with *the freak*! You refuse to tell me what happened and why you're going back. It's like you don't trust me anymore. It's like you don't care about me anymore."

"Kara, I love you. Someday, when I get land grants as an officer, we can be together far away from anyone, just you and me. I trust you, but this is a secret that can't be shared. It's for your safety and mine."

Kara's eyes bored into Dixon like a mek laser. "If you really love me, if you really trust me, stop hanging around that freak and tell me what's going on. Or else…or else we are done."

Dixon felt like he had been punched in the gut by a lug. He grabbed both of Kara's hands and held them tightly. "Kara. I can't. Please understand."

Kara changed her weight to a hippophant and came crashing down from the ceiling toward the floor. Caught by surprise, Dixon still held her hands and came crashing down with her. A few feet from the ground, Kara changed her weight back to a feather and landed gracefully, while Dixon was thrown to the floor.

"Don't you ever touch me or talk to me again," Kara hissed.

She turned and walked out of the auditorium, failing to control her sobs as she put her facemask and gloves back on.

***

She was taller than most female primes, aside from eidetics, and was slender, fitting comfortably into her green uniform signifying a vibrunt in the Ethos Army. The only things missing were her boots. Captain Solsti always walked barefoot.

"Close your eyes...take deep breaths...now clear your mind and focus on the ringed complex of Mount Fegorio," Captain Solsti spoke in hypnotic tones. The exotic woman, with her tall and slender green body, long green hair, and piercing green eyes, paced barefoot in slow circles around Aidan as he sat cross-legged in the center of the room.

"Feel the waves in the air and the earth," she continued gently. "Hear the sounds pulsing around you...don't forget your breathing...deep breaths."

Aidan took deeper breaths. Captain Solsti's words had a calming effect, helping him push aside his racing thoughts about Sim 299, Lieutenant Henderson, and his recent arguments with Fig and Palomas.

"Very good...I can see your heart rate dropping...now reach out with your mind...tell me how far you can see and what you can hear."

Aidan placed his palms on the floor. His entire body transformed into a sensitive antenna, picking up the invisible waves and vibrations buzzing all around him. His mind created a visual blueprint of Captain Solsti's classroom, then the hallway outside, followed by the ring of the second level of the complex. His mind focused on Fig and Palomas, and immediately his senses picked them out as they whispered to each other in their quire programming class.

"I see Fig and Palomas. They're talking about me. They're still upset and worried about me. We fought this morning after I missed our practice time for the trials. I had gone to meet with Dixon and Zana to prepare for Sim 299. But Fig and Palomas didn't care. They think I'm ignoring them and too good for them now," Aidan said, his breaths turning rapid and stifled. "But I'm not ignoring them. They just don't understand. I can't—"

Captain Solsti cut him off with a soft touch to his shoulder. "Relax, Aidan…deep breaths…you cannot fix your friends' feelings from here…move past your friends and push farther into the beauty of the world…push your senses past the other levels of the complex and outside the volcano…in order to see this far, you must relax and focus…and breathe."

Aidan reluctantly pulled his mind away from Fig and Palomas. He took deep breaths, swallowing huge mouthfuls of oxygen, slowly releasing the leftover carbon dioxide through his nose.

"Good…now push farther, go outside the complex," Captain Solsti said calmly. Her rich voice carried a melodic vibration that created a soothing effect on Aidan. When she spoke, he could not refuse. He pushed his senses further. He saw the other two levels of the complex, with cadets, instructors, and staff moving around in their various rooms. He felt outside the metal walls of the complex and touched the black rock of the volcano. Soon he was looking down into the large empty bowl of the dormant volcanic cone, sensing every crack and fissure as his mind spread down the outside walls of the volcano and into the thick jungle surrounding it.

None of the other primes had ever seen outside the metal walls of the Mount Fegorio complex. This was only the second time his vibruntcy had reached the edge of the jungle surrounding the volcano. Captain Solsti had been pushing him lately, prodding and testing his limits. She encouraged him to look and see as far as possible.

"I see the red and black sides of Mount Fegorio and the jungle," Aidan spoke calmly. "The sky is blue today with white puffy clouds, and a flock of spidergeese is flying in a V-formation to the south."

"Very good, Aidan…now try and enter the jungle…relax and move into its green canopy…tell me…what is it like?"

Aidan's mind strained to keep the visual as he pushed into the thick foliage. He cringed.

"Sounds. There are so many sounds. Clicking, ticking, scratching, rustling leaves. And the beasts. There are so many living things. Beasts of every kind. I can't control it. There's too much…"

His heart began to race and his breathing staggered as thousands of images and sounds from the jungle began intermixing with his vision of the volcano and levels of the complex. His vibruntcy struggled to weave all this new data together, creating an incomprehensible mess in his mind.

"Focus, Aidan," Captain Solsti's sweet voice sang in the distance. "Remove the distractions…remove the background noise…see if you can push further…what else can you see?"

Aidan tried to focus, but the noises and images were overwhelming, like having thousands of burning beetlants swarming in his head. This was the furthest he had ever pushed his vibruntcy, and now she wanted him to push further?

"I can't," he whimpered. "It's too much."

"Yes, you can," Captain Solsti calmly reassured him. "Let your incredible mind do the work."

At her words of encouragement, puzzler mode flashed. It melded with his vibruntcy, processing all of the sights and sounds exploding in his mind. His vision cleared, and his breathing returned to normal.

Like being shot from a plasma cannon, his vision sped through the jungle, taking note of every detail, before passing into a massive city on the other side. He swept through skyscrapers and buildings with thousands of people and machines in motion. But still his mind pushed forward. Past the edge of the city he entered a great ocean teeming with life. His mind sped across the ocean to islands and finally to other lands. He saw more cities, mountains, grasslands, other ringed complexes on volcanoes, deserts, icelands, and more. His mind wrapped itself entirely around the vast world of Ethos.

Back in Captain Solsti's classroom, Aidan's body fell to the ground and shuddered. He let out a long moan, and Captain Solsti rushed to his side.

"Aidan. Are you okay?" she called anxiously. "Aidan, can you hear me?"

He gave no response. His chest stopped moving. He was not breathing.

In his mind, Aidan watched the world of Ethos with awe. It was beautiful and amazing. His mind settled on it for only a moment longer before his vision continued pushing outward, leaving Ethos as it entered the blackness of space. He sped toward the orange sun of their system, the green and blue color of Ethos relegated to a small speck in the distance. He passed Omori on the right, noting the dark blue planet's distinguishable white rings, and then sped dizzily through the center of the sun and out to the other side of the Univi star system.

Looking ahead he saw a massive, dark brown planet quickly approaching. It was Hashmeer, the largest of the three planets in the system. His mind dove through the planet's atmosphere and into a lightless city filled with decay. He flinched as he passed hundreds of Splicers standing like statues throughout the city. His vision passed the reptilian sentinels and flew into a tall, domed building at the center of the city.

His vision came to a stop. He was standing in a large room with columns and tall archways around the perimeter. Above him was a high vaulted ceiling with a large dome. Broken stained-glass windows surrounded the dome, letting colorful beams of fading sunlight enter the dark hall. Though dimly lit, his vision remained clear, and his attention turned to the center of the great hall. There he found an all-black Splicer, larger than any Aidan had ever seen, sitting on a black, throne-like chair. The Splicer's eyes were closed, and his head slumped forward.

He wore a black helmet, almost like a crown, connected to dozens of wires extending outward from the throne and into the darkness of the great hall.

As if aware of Aidan's presence, the Splicer raised his scaly, pointed face and his yellow eyes shot open, staring at Aidan from across space. Rearing back his head, the Splicer King released a powerful shriek that filled Aidan's mind with terror and confusion. His vibruntcy sucked him backward, rushing him away from Hashmeer, through the sun, past Omori and retreating him back through the lands of Ethos.

In the blink of an eye, he was back in Captain Solsti's classroom. His green and gray eyes opened as he gasped for air.

"Aidan. Oh, thank Ethos! Are you okay?"

Captain Solsti was cradling him in her long green arms like a newly injected infant. Aidan continued to suck in big breaths of air. His body felt like it was drowning as he struggled for oxygen. It was a sensation he knew all too well from some of his previous deaths in the simulations. After several minutes, his breathing relaxed and he nodded.

"I'm okay."

Captain Solsti's usual calming voice was replaced by anxious tones and hurried questions. "What happened? What did you see? You stopped breathing for close to a minute, but when I scanned your body, your vitals were still fine. I thought you were dead. Are you sure you're okay?"

Aidan sat up while Captain Solsti fetched him a drink of water.

"I'm fine," he tried to reassure her. "My vision, it went everywhere. I saw…everything."

Aidan explained his vision in detail. He noticed her green skin turn a shade paler as he described Hashmeer and the black Splicer with the crown.

"That's impossible, Aidan. I can only see into the jungle from here, and that's only after I've been meditating for hours. What you're describing can't be real."

But it was real, and Aidan knew it.

"What do you think it all means?" Aidan asked.

"I'm not sure. You should probably discuss it with Estra-, I mean General Estrago. If anyone has information to help, it will be him."

Aidan nodded. He would talk with the general tonight.

Captain Solsti cocked her head sideways toward the door, her green, blind eyes staring off into the distance. "I believe we have a visitor."

Captain Solsti tapped her quire processor and opened the door. "Come in, Lieutenant Henderson," she said before the man pushed the door buzzer. "How can I help you?"

The old lieutenant pulled back his finger from the buzzer and gave a sheepish smile.

"Lieutenant, sir," Aidan said with a half-hearted salute, still feeling a little weak from his recent vibrunt vision.

What is he doing here? Aidan thought. *Shouldn't he be preparing to teach Fig's class on mek inventions?*

Lieutenant Henderson walked into the room and gave a slight bow of the head, revealing a patch of baldness at the center of his close-cut gray hair.

"Hello, Captain Solsti. I'm sorry to interrupt your lesson, but I actually came to see Aidan. May I speak with him for a moment?" he asked in a subdued voice.

Captain Solsti pulled back a few green wisps of hair dangling in front of her face and nodded. "Very well, I shall leave you two alone for a moment."

Lieutenant Henderson pulled at his collar with one hand and tapped his fingers against his leg with the other. He shook his head. "Uhmm…on second thought…could you please stay Captain Solsti? After all the help you've given me, this apology is intended as much for you as it is for Aidan."

The confrontation in Lieutenant Henderson's class, only three days before, had spread like wildfire among the cadets. Word of the incident reached the other master officers including the headmaster, General Estrago, and rumor was Lieutenant Henderson's position was under review.

"Aidan, I owe you a deep and sincere apology. I am sorry for how I treated you and your coterie. My actions were childish, horrific, and wrong. I lost control of my emotions and gave in to an angry rage that has been boiling in me for years. You and your coterie were simply the unlucky recipients when I snapped. My actions were unbecoming of an officer and a master instructor in the

Ethos Army. There was only one master in the room that morning—you. I want to thank you for saving my life and for the respect you showed me. I hope you will accept my apology."

Lieutenant Henderson wringed his hands as he waited for an answer. His hair looked grayer and his body frail.

Has he lost weight? Aidan thought.

Aidan looked to Captain Solsti, who simply nodded her head encouragingly.

Aidan offered his hand to Lieutenant Henderson. "I accept, sir."

A look of relief swept across Lieutenant Henderson's peachy face. He eagerly took Aidan's hand and exchanged a firm, but friendly, handshake.

"Thank you," Lieutenant Henderson said. "You don't know how much this means to me."

Aidan felt the sincerity of the lieutenant's words—he saw the man's original distress, followed by relief at being forgiven—but still a question gnawed at Aidan's insides.

"Lieutenant Henderson, *sir,*" he said, making sure to emphasize the *sir* out of fear the man's kindness would only extend so far. "May I ask, why do you serve the Ethos Army when it's clear you hate primes so much?"

Lieutenant Henderson bit his lip and folded his arms. "My, the boy does get right to the heart of things, doesn't he?" Lieutenant Henderson said to Captain Solsti with a shaky laugh.

"That he does," Captain Solsti agreed in her melodic tone.

Aidan simply looked at the lieutenant and waited for an answer. What would drive a man to serve among people he hates?

Taking a note from Captain Solsti's book, Lieutenant Henderson took a deep breath and slowly released it. "It's complicated. I love this world and want to defend it. And it's not that I hate primes, just what many of them are doing. You've never seen the outside of this complex before, so it may be hard for you to comprehend."

Aidan gave Captain Solsti a knowing glance, remembering how mere minutes ago his mind had allowed him to see a giant Splicer in the center of Hashmeer, on the other side of the Univi star system.

Lieutenant Henderson turned his head to the side and coughed, his cheeks turning slightly red as he did. "In the outside world, humans, like myself, are often treated as second-class citizens by the primes. There are many abuses by local prime peace officers and the military force. Humans are forced to work like slaves, building war machines and harvesting the plants and minerals used to supply the food printers. Then there is the matter of our children…"

Lieutenant Henderson's voice caught in his throat. "Tell me Aidan, do you know how you came to be here? Do you understand how primes are chosen?"

Aidan nodded. It was an easy question. "We are chosen because our genetic code is a match for the Prime

Injection. It's our duty as genetic matches to be injected and join the Ethos Army."

Lieutenant Henderson nodded his head, the color rising in his cheeks again. He stared at Aidan remorsefully, his eyes a mixture of pity and sadness.

"Yes, that is how you are chosen, but sometimes the sacrifice is greatest for your parents," said Lieutenant Henderson.

He paused for a moment, taking a few more deep breaths before continuing. "As you can see, I harbor some dissonance with our current leadership. Perhaps it is for the best that I have been effectively relieved of duty and stripped of my ranking as an officer. I will no longer be a master instructor at Mount Fegorio and will not be able to cause any more problems here."

Captain Solsti gasped. "Oh, Joshua. How could they? After all you've sacrificed. I never expected such harsh punishment."

"It came straight from the Director," Lieutenant Henderson said. "I met with General Estrago this morning and he informed me of the decision. I'm just thankful to be alive. General Estrago said the Director was furious with my actions and the only thing keeping me from execution was my longtime service on the Omori battlefront.

"To be honest, this is a blessing in disguise. Trying to instruct and manage a classroom full of teenagers is a taxing proposition for an old goatmole like me, especially when I have no abilities to help enforce discipline and my students are hormone-raging primes with superpowers.

Giving up teaching will be good for my health and my blood pressure." He managed a small smile.

"But what will you do?" asked Captain Solsti.

The aging man shrugged his shoulders. "Don't worry about me. I have a cousin in Vapor City. He runs a bipod repair shop and offered me a job as a mechanic. I'll be fine. But, Aidan, I want to you to know, if you ever need anything after you graduate, look me up. I will be happy to help. I owe you a hundredfold not only for forgiving me, but for saving my life."

Aidan nodded. The change over Lieutenant Henderson was like night and day. The anger seething under his skin, and the hard-nosed persona he normally wore, were gone. He appeared lighter and happier now that the burden of teaching was lifted from his shoulders.

"I must be off now. Security is escorting me to Vapor City shortly. Goodbye."

"Goodbye, Lieutenant Henderson, sir," Aidan said with a salute.

Lieutenant Henderson waved off the salute. "I'm no longer a lieutenant, my boy. You can call me Joshua. My full name is Joshua Michael Henderson. Full names are something else taken away from primes," he harrumphed. "Your true names are stripped away when you are conscripted as newborns and replaced with a new, single name. It's meant to break your ties to your past. But, alas, I digress. Farewell and good luck to you, Aidan."

Henderson gave Aidan another firm handshake, and Captain Solsti wrapped the man in a friendly hug before showing him to the door.

When she came back, Aidan gave her a puzzled look.

"You asked him to come here, didn't you?"

Captain Solsti smiled at Aidan's directness. "Yes," she said. "You're a smart boy. How did you know?"

Aidan grinned. "I heard you say so when you whispered to him at the door just now. I'm a vibrunt too, you know."

Captain Solsti rolled her blind, green eyes. "Eavesdropping is not polite young man. But you are correct, I did ask him to come by today. Sadly, I had no idea he had been relieved of duty. Lieut—I mean, Joshua—has been disgusted with himself ever since the incident in his class. Over the last year he's been meeting with me for meditation lessons to help him control his anger. He's felt sick, and hasn't eaten a thing since he lost control on you and your coterie. What he did was wrong, and I do not condone it, but his actions were not those of the man I have come to know. He needed your forgiveness as much as you needed to hear his apology."

Aidan's emotions flowed in every direction. He still felt the awe of the vision, the fear of the Splicer King, the anger toward Lieutenant Henderson, and now a deep sadness for the man.

"You called him Joshua. Is it true what he said about our names being taken away? Do you know what my real names are?"

Captain Solsti shook her head. "No. I don't even know what my true names were."

"Is there some way I can find out? Who would know my names?"

Captain Solsti sighed softly. "That information is secured somewhere, but I do not know where. Your name is Aidan now, and it is a good name because you are a good person, not the other way around."

"Why haven't I heard that Lieutenant, I mean Joshua, made sacrifices in the war? What did you mean? What sacrifices has he made?"

Captain Solsti sat on a hard metal chair across from Aidan and closed her blind eyes as she spoke.

"Joshua was once a major general. He had command over all the human engineering corps on the planet Omori. That made him the highest-ranking human in the Ethos Army. He was serving on the front lines when his second child was born, a baby boy. His first child, a girl, had the proper genetics and was chosen for the Prime Initiative immediately after birth. Reluctantly, he and his wife gave her up, seeing it as their duty to provide a prime candidate like other human families. They were shocked to find out his second child also had the prime gene, as it was rare to manifest in multiple children. Unable to bear losing another child, his wife took one of her husband's laser cannons, which he kept hidden in their home, and fired it on the primes that came to extract the baby. She killed a lug and an eidetic doctor before she was subdued and taken prisoner.

"When he heard the news, Joshua abandoned his command, resigning as the top-ranking human in the Ethos Army. He hurried home on the next transport ship to defend his wife during her trial. She was executed three days before his flight returned home."

Aidan shook his head. His mind was at a loss and he hardly noticed the single tear trickling down his cheeks. "That's awful," he whispered.

"I agree," Captain Solsti replied in her calming voice. "But instead of giving up, he applied to become a master instructor at Mount Fegorio and received the lowest rank required to teach. He was demoted to a lieutenant. He would never admit it, but I think he hoped he would find his children, or at least teach them in his classes. From what he's told me, they would be about your age. But the chances of him finding them would be slim. He would never know who they were, what they looked like, what complex they were sent to, what power they possessed, or if they even survived the injection. But he hoped he would see them again. Sometimes hope is all we have."

GOATMOLE

CHAPTER 8: HISTORY

Originally the Prime Initiative was designed as a master vaccine to prolong human life and act as a cure-all against every manner of disease and virus. Our research found that the keys to unlock these natural protections were hidden in the complexities of our own minds.

—Doctor T.M. Omori,
Man's Quest for Destruction: A Case for the Prime Initiative

Aidan, Palomas and Fig walked into General Estrago's History of Warfare course. None of them were speaking or signing to each other.

Aidan had missed yet another practice for their upcoming trial, and Palomas was fuming. Fig couldn't understand why Aidan was spending more time with Dixon and Zana—especially Zana, whom Fig considered his mortal enemy—than he was with his own brother and sister.

Aidan was tiring of these arguments, and he lacked the patience for them. Every time they spoke, it turned into a fight about why Aidan couldn't share his experience in Sim 299, and why he kept missing trial practice.

If only they would understand! Aidan thought. He, Dixon and Zana were too busy trying to build upgrades to take with them into the sim, in addition to Aidan's research on dragleons, which had yielded nothing so far.

But Palomas and Fig didn't understand. How could they? That was part of the reason Aidan had kept yesterday's experience of melding vibruntcy-puzzler mode in Captain Solsti's class a secret. He had no desire to tell them about his vision of Hashmeer and the Splicer King. With how they were communicating with each other lately, it would probably turn into another argument.

Aidan sat down first and was further agitated when Fig and Palomas decided to sit four chairs down from him, instead of taking their usual seats at his side.

General Estrago's History of Warfare course was different from other classes since all upper coteries, age twelve to sixteen, took the class together each year. Apparently General Estrago gave the same lessons each year, citing the history of the war and the strategies of key battles both won and lost. The idea was that by the time a prime cadet graduated, the repeated information would not only be remembered, but would be engrained in their thought process as they planned and carried out future battles against the Splicers.

With no one sitting near Aidan, Dixon and Zana pulled up the chairs at his side. Aidan watched as Fig and Palomas gave the three of them dirty looks. To his right, Aidan watched Kara and her fifteen-year minions follow her to seats near the front of the classroom. She also turned her attention toward Aidan, Dixon and Zana. Though she was still masked, Aidan had the distinct impression she was trying to shoot laser beams from her eyes to annihilate the three of them.

"Good thing agulators don't have laser vision as a power," Aidan whispered to Dixon, who was also following Kara's stare.

"Tell me about it," Dixon whispered back mournfully.

General Estrago entered the room, and all the prime cadets stood at attention and saluted.

"At ease," General Estrago said, and flicked on the large holovid at the front of the class.

"You will all have a test next week on what we have learned in the first portion of this upper-coterie class. Today, I would like to review how the Splicer War originated and the first battle of Hashmeer."

A few of the seniors, including Zana, and a handful of eidetics groaned. Aidan felt for them. The seniors had suffered through this class for five years, and the eidetics had it all memorized after hearing it the first time.

"To begin, who can explain how our ancestors first arrived in this, the Univi star system?"

A tall eidetic boy, Garth, raised his hand. He was the fifteen-year coterie eidetic Aidan had hit with the bearcat dung and burning beetlants in the first trial. Aidan grimaced as he remembered the pain he caused the boy.

"Our ancestors travelled here 263 years ago from the original colonial world of Justus. Over 13,000 people arrived on the three Advanced Relocation Carrier Starships, known as the ARCs, to settle the three habitable worlds. That marks year 1 a.a., or year 1 of the ARCs Arrival. The worlds our ancestors inhabited were named after the chief scientists on each of the three starships—doctors Ethos, Omori and Hashmeer."

"Correct. Thank you Cadet Garth. Your eidetic recall is perfect," General Estrago said. Garth beamed at the praise, his already elongated neck stretching a bit higher with pride.

"From this point, can someone explain how the Splicer War began?"

Garth's hand shot up again, along with a handful of other eidetics.

"How about someone who is not an eidetic?" General Estrago asked, eyeing the rest of the class.

Beside Aidan, Dixon raised his hand into the air.

"Yes, Cadet Dixon," General Estrago called. "Tell us how the war began."

"After the worlds were settled, they began to grow and populate," Dixon replied. "In 45 a.a., a hidden force of Splicers invaded Hashmeer. Eventually, they overran the planet and Hashmeer was lost."

This rubbed on Aidan. He had yet to discuss his vibrunt vision of the Splicer King with General Estrago. The general had sent Aidan away the previous night, claiming he was too busy with his research to talk with him. This left Aidan annoyed. He had questions that needed answers, and the watered-down history Dixon was repeating didn't have those answers.

"What does a Splicer look like?" Aidan interrupted without raising his hand. He knew he shouldn't ask these questions now, but between the stresses of his inevitable return to Sim 299, the arguments with Palomas and Fig and his mysterious vibrunt vision, Aidan didn't care. He wanted answers now, and he poured his frustrations into his questions.

"Why don't we have any pictures or battle footage of the Splicers to study? You would think it would be at least a *little* important to study them before we go into battle."

The brown in General Estrago's cheeks flushed darker. He looked at Aidan and frowned. "As you very well know, Cadet Aidan, that information is classified, and you will receive full briefings on such topics after graduating and arriving on the planet Omori."

"But that makes little tactical sense," Aidan continued, before General Estrago could move on with his lesson. "We should know what we're up against and train for it. How else are we expected to fight them and win?"

General Estrago frowned again. "You don't have to understand it, *Cadet*. You only have to follow your orders. This specific order about withholding knowledge of the Splicers is the direct decree of *Director Tuskin,"* General Estrago said, as if that settled the matter.

Other cadets whispered in hushed voices at the mention of the Director.

But Aidan was not done. "Can you at least tell us what color the Splicers are? I hear they look like giant lizard men and are usually green. Have you ever heard of an all-black Splicer? Do the Splicers have a leader? A king maybe?"

Fig, Palomas and the rest of the class looked at him like he was crazy. Exasperated with the string of questions, General Estrago released a low growl and shook his head with annoyance.

"Cadet Aidan," he said sharply. "You seem to have quite the imaginative questions today. Perhaps, instead of interrupting this class, you should reread the course book on your quire processor *tonight* and write down these strange questions of yours on your own time, *tonight*."

Aidan harrumphed. "I tried doing that *last* night, but apparently things were *too busy*."

General Estrago frowned again, pulling his lips tight as he stared at Aidan.

Aidan knew he was not going to get any answers now, and upsetting General Estrago would not help his cause later that night, but he felt surprisingly better after putting General Estrago on the hot seat and letting out some of his frustrations.

General Estrago was about to speak when Aidan cut him off. "I'll take your advice and try to write my questions down again," Aidan said. "Perhaps I will have more success *tonight*."

General Estrago grunted, his face still frowning. "Perhaps you will. Now if you are done interrupting this class, let us continue."

Aidan leaned back in his chair, silent, as the class discussion moved on to the topic of the failed embargo of Hashmeer.

***

After General Estrago's class, Aidan, Dixon and Zana walked together to the commissary for lunch. It had been two weeks since Sentinel released them from the Pit and warned they must return. They spent every free minute together planning their upgrades and strategizing how to defeat Sim 299, much to the angst of their own coteries and friends. Their planning seemed futile at times, since they had no idea what to expect in the sim, but they were soldiers, and strategizing brought them a small amount of comfort as they prepared for the unknown.

While they built their upgrades, they discussed battle tactics and experiences from past sims, and took turns making up wild scenarios about what they might face. But even this did not quench the nervousness they felt as the reentry day approached.

"Guys, I've thought long and hard the last two weeks, and I've decided I don't want to go back to Sim 299," Zana protested as she retied her blue hair into a ponytail. "Have you seen Wesley? He's still not quite right in the head after dying in the acid moat. I think I would rather live without my quire than be brain-damaged the rest of my life."

"He was never right in the head," Dixon retorted. "Besides, Aidan has died in there hundreds of times and you don't see him complaining. Remember what Sentinel said: *Pain is a teacher.*"

Though they had grown closer since their experience in the sim, Dixon's compliment still caught Aidan off guard. Only weeks ago the senior had threatened him, warning him to 'watch his back.' Ironically, that's exactly what Dixon and Zana were doing in Sim 299—watching Aidan's back.

Dixon lifted a sandwich in his white-gloved hand and used his other hand to peel back the bottom of his mask to reveal his mouth. He quickly took a large bite, his white lips closing around the food, and put the bottom of his mask back over his sharply angled chin and thick neck. Even though the complex was protected from UV rays, all agulators were trained to obey the first agulator rule—never remove your safety gear unless absolutely necessary. It was a protection to them at all times in case of an emergency. That meant they even slept in their white agulator uniforms.

"Of course," Dixon said between bites, his mask back on, "all of Aidan's deaths in Sim 299 might explain why he's such a weirdo," Dixon joked playfully, elbowing Aidan in the ribs. Aidan punched Dixon's arm in retaliation. He found it kind of nice to make friends with someone else besides Fig and Palomas, not that he didn't like or miss them. They were his family, and he loved them, but hanging out with Dixon and Zana was a nice change. Plus, it beat getting picked on by Dixon.

"So," Zana asked between mouthfuls of her own sandwich. "Any luck getting your puzzler mode to work again or learning more about dragleon lore?"

Aidan hesitated, not sure if he should share his across-star-system vision with them. He opted against it, deciding it best to first talk about it with General Estrago that night.

"Nothing yet," Aidan answered, feeling slightly guilty for lying.

"Did someone say *dragleons*?" Fig asked, surprising the trio from behind. He and Palomas took a seat at the table with Aidan, Dixon, and Zana. "Why do you need to know about dragleons?"

Dixon and Zana eyed the pair suspiciously. It had been difficult to keep their secret from their own coterie, but they worried more about Aidan. If Aidan broke the silence rule and was banned from the sim, they did not stand a chance on their own.

"Uhmm, no reason," Aidan answered hesitantly.

Palomas gave Aidan the evil eye. "Maybe, instead of discussing fake monsters with these two, you should put more effort into helping us plan for our trial this evening. In case you haven't noticed, we've been demolished in the last two trials. Our coterie is in second-to-last place with only one win."

Fig shoved in a mouthful of food from the towering pile of delicacies on his plate. His cheeks bulged like a snailmunk as he chewed with his mouth open and spoke. "Hey, if we win the next two trials, we have a shot at the finals."

"You guys will never win," Zana sneered.

"And why not?" Fig argued.

Zana arched one of her razor-thin eyebrows. "Simple: because you would have to face us in the championship. The senior primes are undefeated."

Fig rolled his eyes and snickered.

"Aidan, you need to get your head in the game," Palomas signed. "I would like to avoid being smashed by another boulder, electrocuted by meks or chased by another swarm of burning beetlants because you were not focused. You're our leader and we need you ready."

Aidan grimaced as he remembered the painful ordeals Palomas described from the last two trials, especially the burning beetlants. All of the coteries had weaponized them after watching his use of them in their first trial. Palomas was right, though—he should have seen all of those attacks with his vibruntcy, but he wasn't focused. But what could he do? Puzzler mode still wasn't working, and their reentry into Sim 299 was one week away. Sim 299 was simply more important. He couldn't take time to prepare for the trials.

"Whoa, relax missy," Zana said to Palomas. "Give the guy a break. He's got a lot on his plate. We're up against some craziness that we can't share with anyone, so cut him some slack."

Fig made a fist. "Hey! No one tells my sister to relax, and no one calls her missy except me. Especially a mek with a second-rate suit."

Zana narrowed her eyes and stood on top of her chair to lean over the table toward Fig. "Excuse me? Second-rate suit? Alright little man, you better be ready for the Zana Attackana!"

"*Little man?*" Fig retorted, standing up in his own chair. "I'm as tall as you are!"

Aidan couldn't shake the uncanny resemblance between the two blue meks as they faced off from their chairs.

"For your insults," Fig continued, "I give Palomas permission to break both your arms."

Fig snapped his small fingers, and Palomas rose from her seat to reach across the table and grab Zana.

Zana jumped backward off her chair, and Dixon quickly moved between the two.

"*STOP IT!*" Aidan shouted.

Everyone in the commissary turned to watch the commotion.

"Fig. Palomas," he whispered sharply, trying to avoid drawing further attention to themselves. "You're my family and I need you to trust me. I'm sorry about the trials, but we need to stop these petty arguments now. Like Zana said, we have a lot on our plates right now."

"Not as much as Fig," Zana joked, gesturing toward Fig's overflowing plate of food as she doubled over in laughter at her own joke.

Fig's plate was piled high with random cuisines that were never intended to be eaten together, and it smelled equally unappetizing.

"Zana. Cool it," Dixon barked.

Zana rolled her eyes and made a face at Fig, who returned the gesture with his own contorted blue face.

"Listen. For what it's worth, I'm sorry about this too," Dixon offered. "To be honest, I used to hate you guys, especially Aidan, but I was wrong. He saved my life in Sim 299, and what he's telling you is true. We can't share what happened with anyone or there could be severe consequences. This is tough on all of us, not just you two."

Dixon glanced longlingly across the room towards Kara. She sat two tables down from them with her own coterie. He had tried to reach out to her, but she had completely ignored him since her ultimatum in the auditorium.

Palomas blew out an exasperated breath. "Fine," she signed. "But we know you are planning to go back into Sim 299 in a few days. We want to help. What can we do?"

Dixon and Zana gave Aidan a troubled look.

"Don't look at me. I didn't say anything," Aidan quickly denied.

"Neither did we," Dixon responded.

Fig shook his head. "You guys should really stick to communicating in sign language," he chastised, pulling out his vibrunt ears. "We've heard almost everything you three have been planning for the last two weeks, and we are going to help whether you like it or not."

Zana's eyes bulged at the sight of the new tech. "No way! Those things look sweet. Can I see them?" she begged, pointing toward the vibrunt ears.

Dixon slapped Zana's hand, silencing her. New tech always sent meks into a frenzy. Turning back to Fig and Palomas, Dixon leaned in close until his white masked face was inches away from theirs. "I can't believe you've been eavesdropping on us! Do you know what you've done?!" he hissed.

Aidan pulled Dixon back. "Relax. Technically, we didn't tell them anything. We should be safe. But since you guys know what's going on, there are a few things I've been wishing I could talk to you about and ask for your help. We only have one week until we have to return to the sim and the new tech we've been working on to use in the sim isn't ready yet. But let's not talk about it here. How about we all go back to my room. Agreed?"

Everyone nodded, though Fig looked at his plate somewhat disturbed. He rapidly shoveled fistfuls of food down his throat while the others stared at him.

"What? I'm a growing mek," he said between bites. "I can't let this food go to waste."

Aidan rolled his eyes and couldn't help but smile. He had missed his friend and brother during the last two weeks. Avoiding him on purpose to ensure he did not reveal any secrets had been difficult. It was a relief that they could be close again. He just hoped his coterie would play nice with Dixon and Zana.

After Fig devoured his lunch in less than a minute, the group made their way to Aidan's room, where Aidan tapped his quire to flip off the security cameras.

He explained what they needed from Fig and Palomas.

"We only have one week to get it all done. And Palomas, you only have one day to take care of your main part. Any questions?"

Fig shrugged. "Seems doable. I only wish we could go in there with you."

"Me too," Aidan answered.

An alarm went off on Dixon's quire processor. "We better get moving. Lunch is over in two minutes and I can't be late to class again."

Dixon slid the door open to leave and suddenly jumped backward a step.

"What the batmonkeys!" he swore in surprise.

The massive form of General Estrago stood behind the door, filling the entryway.

"Uhmm, General Estrago, sir." Dixon hastily recovered, coming to attention. The rest of the cadets followed suit and saluted the general.

General Estrago gave a slight nod of recognition, seemingly unsurprised to see Dixon and Zana in Aidan's room. "Pardon the interruption," he said in his deep voice, gently pulling on his beard with one hand. "But there is a matter of urgency that must be addressed."

The young primes eyed one another, wondering what General Estrago knew about their preparations for Sim 299.

"I shall get right to the point. Cadets Aidan, Palomas, and Fig, I would like to introduce you to the newest member of your coterie."

General Estrago stepped into the room, revealing a boy with scarlet skin standing behind him in the doorway. The boy looked about Aidan's age and had fiery red hair that stood straight up like a flame. He wore a red Ethos Army uniform and his face was a mask of seriousness. The only hint of emotion he showed was a slight arch of his left eyebrow as his eyes scanned the room, taking in Aidan and his fellow cadets.

"This is Masay. As you can see, he is a vigori. Very rare. He has been transferred here from one of our distant training facilities in the north, specifically to join your coterie. I ask that you take him to class with you and help him become acquainted with Mount Fegorio. Treat him as one of your own, since he is now an official member of your coterie."

General Estrago paused to let the news settle while Aidan, Fig and Palomas stood stunned.

"I understand you have another trial this evening," General Estrago continued. "Masay should prove quite the asset during your battles."

Masay did not smile or frown, trying to keep a serious face. His bright red hair, uniform, and skin stood out against the gray walls of Aidan's room like a burning flame.

Palomas narrowed her eyes. The newcomer commanded attention. Without saying a word, she could tell he was a natural leader. He reminded her of Aidan, but different. There was no gentleness in eyes.

"Hello," Masay said, offering his hand to Aidan. "It's good to meet you."

SNAILMUNK

CHAPTER 9: MASAY

This rebellion against the primes has become a distraction to our government that can no longer be ignored. At one point in my life, I may have sided with the rebels and their values, but now I believe their rebellion must be crushed.

—Doctor T.M. Omori,
Man's Quest for Destruction: A Case for the Prime Initiative

irector Tuskin grinned. He did not smile anymore. His satisfied grin was as close as he came to smiling in his old age.

The latest report from his secret team of elite hackers had yielded promising results from their last test. The new member of Aidan's coterie had been transferred successfully and his army of primes on the planet Omori had regained ground from the Splicers and were finally on the offensive.

Everything was falling into place.

The only loose end remaining was the rebels. He grudgingly admired their ability to remain hidden from his view. He had put an end to dozens of rebellions during his centuries-long reign as Director, but this latest group had proved quite resourceful—and annoying. Their growing support and recruitment of his primes was disturbing. None of his spies had been able to infiltrate the rebellion, and he knew the reason why.

The Reader, he thought.

A scowl replaced his grin. *I've spent far too many years bringing order and unity to this planet to let it be threatened by this…rebellion,* the Director thought angrily.

An idea came to his mind. His skin flashed brown, and his eidetic memory pulled in years of stored information that he used to nourish the idea and help it grow until it matured into a calculated plan.

"Yes," he whispered—his grin returning. "Yes, I believe that will work nicely."

**

Aidan sat across the desk from General Estrago and shook his head. "But you agreed, in your class today, that our ancestors' pilgrimage to this star system was to colonize it. They arrived on the ARCs and a few years later, the Splicers came and the war broke out. But now you're telling me we actually came to the Univi system because we were running away from the Splicers to begin with?"

"You have not been reading your book, have you?" General Estrago asked disapprovingly.

Aidan pursed his lips and squinted his eyes. "I've read a little bit. But I've been kind of busy lately."

General Estrago sighed. "You really should read the book. I'm only giving you a cursory introduction to this information. T.M. Omori's book is the closest text I've encountered to a true history of the Splicer War and our prime heritage."

"So if we were running away from the Splicers, where did they come from? Do they have a home world? What system are they from? Why are they attacking us?"

"The text is unclear on those matters," General Estrago said. "We know little, if anything, of their origins. But we do know that we can never return to our home system, even if we wanted to. The cores on the ARCs were completely drained, and we have no means of resupplying them with the resources in our current system. It appears our ancestors planned a one-way trip when they came here."

Aidan flipped through the book, *Man's Quest for Destruction: A Case for the Prime Initiative*. In all honesty, he had not cracked open the worn green cover at all since the night he received it from General Estrago. He knew he should read it, but he really had been busy with classes and Sim 299. Plus, it did seem really boring. But the new information General Estrago shared piqued his interest. He needed to find out more about the Splicers.

"So what else *can* you tell me about the Splicers? I've already faced one in Sim 299 and you confirmed that my description matches their physiology. What about my vision? Was it real? Have you ever heard of a Splicer King on Hashmeer?"

At these questions, General Estrago stroked his beard and narrowed his eyes. His mind ran through millions of stored memories and information.

"To those questions, I must answer truthfully. I do not know. One man may hold that information, but I doubt he will share his knowledge."

"Who is it?" Aidan asked.

General Estrago frowned and tugged harder on his beard, which in turn pulled the skin and thick scars on his face tighter against his cheekbones. "It's Director Tuskin."

Now Aidan frowned. Everyone feared Director Tuskin and heard the rumors of his workings. But none of it made sense. The man seemed more like a myth than a reality, yet General Estrago had obviously met him and talked with him. If he had so many answers, why hide them? Why hide the true history? Why hide what the Splicers were like? Why hide himself so secretively?

Only one explanation made sense to him: *power and control.*

***

Aidan shivered as he trudged through the thick snowbanks on the side of the mountain valley. He wore the heavy, white camouflage snow gear of the Ethos Army, but the bitter cold still seeped into his bones.

"Fig, Palomas, Masay, do you copy?"

Still, there was no answer. The sim for this trial had landed each participant in random spots of the mountain valley. This was an elimination round, and the objective was simple. The first coterie to capture or kill all members of the other coterie won.

The blinding snowstorm seemed to affect all communication, causing only static on their commlinks. Aidan vibroscanned the area, but the blizzard conditions caused a white-out effect on his vibruntcy as well. The sound of the wind and the whipping movement of millions of snowflakes only allowed him to see a few feet in each direction. Still he focused, trying to process all of the movements and vibrations.

There it is again, he thought. A blip appeared on the three-dimensional view in his mind. It looked like two individuals blazing a trail up ahead, but then they disappeared. He had no idea if they were friend or foe, but there was only one way to find out.

For this trial, they faced the fourteen-year coterie, which had eight total cadets. Once again, they were outmatched by numbers and age.

Aidan worried about Fig and Palomas, but knew they were prepared for the trial. What was more concerning was the introduction of Masay into their coterie. Who was he? Was it coincidence that he showed up days before their jump back into Sim 299? Coterie transfers between complexes were uncommon, but not unheard of. General Estrago once told Aidan there were over six hundred training facilities like Mount Fegorio spread across Ethos. Surely this had to be a coincidence.

Aidan stopped walking, his body knee-deep in powdery snow. His wandering mind caused him to lose focus on his direction and the two life forms he saw moving in the area. He pulled off his glove, shivering as the cold stung his fingertips, and pushed his arm through two feet of snow to touch the icy ground below. He vibroscanned the area again, putting more effort into his vision. He saw nothing.

"Where did those two disappear to?" he whispered.

Aidan pulled his numb fingers back into his glove. Something was not right. He tried to access puzzler mode, but once again it was not cooperating. The desolation and loneliness of the sim was beginning to wreak havoc on his nerves as he trudged through heavy snowbank after heavy snowbank.

How long have I been walking? he thought wearily. Each new step seemed to drain more of his physical and mental energy.

Aidan heard a crunch in the snow behind him and he froze, which was not hard to do in the frigid climate. The blizzard only allowed a few feet of visibility and he saw no one behind him.

"Who's there?" he asked, trying to sound confident through chattering teeth.

Aidan heard another crunch, this time to his side, followed by two, then three more in every direction. A howl went up from only a few feet ahead, followed by a half-dozen more howls in every direction. Slowly the sources of howling came into view. Aidan was surrounded by a pack of wolfstags.

"This is not good," Aidan muttered.

The wolfstags inched closer, step by step. They were a head taller than Aidan—some white, some gray—and their fur blended with the snowy background. Only their dark black noses and sharp black antlers, rising high into the air, made them easily recognizable. The wolfstags bared their fangs and growled menacingly as they enclosed their circle around Aidan.

Aidan's mind raced through his training on wild beasts.

When confronted by a wolfstag pack, one should lie on the ground and play dead, he remembered.

Aidan looked at the encircling pack and thought that was the stupidest advice he had ever heard.

How can you tell if a man devoured by a wolfstag was playing dead? He could have played dead better than anyone else and they still would have eaten him, he thought.

Aidan shook his head, gathering his focus.

"This is only a sim," he said out loud. "If I'm going down now, I'm going down with a fight."

A red blur zoomed into the center of the wolfstag pack and stopped at his side. Aidan blinked to make sure he wasn't hallucinating.

"Masay?" Aidan questioned.

The red-haired vigori nodded and faced the approaching wolfstags. "Follow my lead if you want to live. Your friends need help."

Masay stood on his tip toes, rounded his shoulders and waved his hands high in the air, trying to appear as large as possible. He reared back his head and howled as loudly as possible, sounding eerily similar to the wolfstag howls of the pack. Still unsure of himself, Aidan followed Masay's lead and howled to the sky. He immediately observed that his howl sounded weak and sickly compared to Masay's, but he continued howling nonstop.

Masay turned his attention to the leader of the pack. Clearly this all-white beast, which outmatched the rest of the pack in height and mass, was the alpha male.

Masay growled at the beast, producing vicious guttural noises that scared Aidan and caused him to stop his own howling to the sky.

All of the other wolfstags went silent, taking a step backward from the duo—all except the alpha male, who stood his ground and growled back at Masay.

In the blink of an eye, Masay sprinted to the side of the alpha male, climbed on the beast's back and pulled on the wolfstag's antlers. The alpha male howled in protest and attempted to shake off Masay, but he held fast and produced a piercing howl of his own.

The alpha male shook his head again and again, twisting, turning and jumping into the air. After another minute the beast relented, releasing a steamy breath of air from his black nostrils. Masay patted the neck of the wolfstag and growled at the beast in low, calm tones.

"Choose one," Masay said, waving to the rest of the pack. "Climb on its back and grab its antlers to hold on. Above all, show no fear."

Aidan hesitated, not sure if he had heard Masay correctly and confused by what he had just witnessed.

"Hurry," Masay said. "Fig and Palomas have been captured. They're in a cave about three miles north of here. Follow me."

Aidan threw caution to the frozen wind and mounted a gray wolfstag standing next to Masay. Although his nostrils were frozen, he still caught a faint whiff of musty, wet dog.

At the front of the pack, Masay tugged on the alpha male's antlers and pointed him in the direction of the cave. With a kick of his heels, the wolfstag took off in a sprint. The remaining wolfstags, including the gray beast Aidan found himself uncomfortably perched on, followed close behind their leader. The wind and snow whipped by Aidan's face, but all thought of the cold was replaced by the exhilarating speed of the beasts and the pounding of his heart.

Within a few minutes, the pack came to a halt at the edge of a clearing below them. In the center was a large mound with a single cave entrance. Two lugs, two eidetics and a mek stood guard outside the cave.

Aidan pulled his wolfstag closer to Masay. "How did they find each other so fast? I was wandering around for hours without running into anybody."

"Probably a homing beacon," Masay responded. "We learned how to make them at the Ice Mount as kids for blizzard survival training, but you probably haven't studied it yet. I bet it's in one of the upper-level courses you haven't taken yet."

"And what about this?" Aidan said waving his hands at their wolfstag steeds. "Did you *learn* this too?"

Masay nodded. "I learned this last year from my vigori instructor. He said only vigori can tame a wolfstag. We're fast enough to mount them, and we can vibrate our voices to mimic their growls and howls. Plus, if it doesn't work we can always run away."

"Okay then. Consider me impressed," Aidan remarked, removing himself from the wolfstag's back. The snow was lighter in this area and he removed his hand from his warm glove, pressing it to the icy ground. Aidan could vibroscan an area without touching the earth, but the direct contact with his skin made his vibruntcy clearer and he needed to see what was happening in the cave.

An image of Fig and Palomas, bound in chains, appeared in his vision. Fig's mek suit lay discarded to the side, crushed and dented. Two agulators and a second mek paced in the cave beside them.

"I say we kill them now," said the first agulator, a male.

"I'm with you," said the female voice of the other agulator.

"No," whined the mek from inside his suit. "Do not touch them yet. Their friends will come, and when they do, we will end them all and win the trial. If that freak vibroscans and sees them dead, he won't come here to save them, and then we'll have to go out into that freezing storm to hunt him down."

Aidan pulled out of his vision and turned to Masay. "There are two agulators and a mek inside the cave. Fig and Palomas are unconscious and chained up. They're waiting for us. It's clearly a trap."

Masay simply nodded. "What do you suggest?"

Aidan wrinkled his brow and frowned. *Why is he defaulting to me?* Aidan thought. *He's the one with the superspeed and beastmaster powers. First Fig and Palomas, then Dixon and Zana, and now Masay. Why do they all look to me when they are so much stronger and experienced?*

Despite his own doubts of leadership, Aidan did have an idea.

"Well…are you fast enough to get past those guards?" Aidan asked.

"I think so," Masay answered. "But if they trap me in that cave I can't fight them all."

"Leave that to me and the wolfstag pack. We'll draw them away from the entrance while you run into the cave unnoticed. Find a way to free Fig and Palomas."

"Then what?"

"Get them out of the cave and wake them up. We'll need their help for this to work."

Aidan explained the rest of the plan to Masay, who then dismounted from the alpha male and allowed Aidan to take his place on the back of the lead beast. "Okay boy," Aidan whispered to the wolfstag, rubbing the back of his neck the same way he had seen Masay do. "Let's go cause some chaos."

Masay stood a few paces from the wolfstags and gave Aidan a final nod before disappearing in a blur of speed. Aidan kicked his heels into the alpha male, using the beast's antlers to set them on a path straight toward the guards at the cave.

Aidan howled a loud war cry, and the pack joined him in a chorus of howls. The guards turned their attention to the noise, surprise registering on their faces as the pack of wolfstags charged at them with Aidan riding at the head.

Catching them off guard, the large wolfstags pounced on their quarries, striking the first blow. Aidan jumped off the alpha male, who was clawing a mek he had pinned to the ground. Four of the beasts attacked the two lugs while the other wolfstag attacked one of the eidetics. That left Aidan face-to-face with the last eidetic. The eight-foot tall boy lumbered toward Aidan and swung his meaty fist. Although the eidetic was very large and appeared quite strong, he was not particularly quick.

Aidan ducked below the swing and brought down a hard kick to the side of the eidetic's right knee. The eidetic screamed in pain as his leg collapsed. His cry was

lost in the sounds of the battle unfolding around them.
Hearing the commotion outside the cave, the two
agulators and the second mek emerged at the entrance.
Three of the wolfstags broke off and attacked the
newcomers.

The battle continued with losses on both sides.
Three of the six wolfstags had been killed, crushed by the
blows of the lugs and agulators or shot with lasers from
the mek leader. The opposing coterie had lost both
eidetics, a single lug, and the first mek.

Aidan glimpsed a red blur speeding in and out of
the cave behind the backs of their enemy. The opposing
lug, two agulators and lead mek regrouped at the mouth
of the cave after successfully pushing Aidan and the
wolfstags back. Two of the remaining wolfstags hobbled
to the side of the alpha male, their fur stained with blood.

A blur of red rushed toward Aidan and came to
halt. "They're both out and awake. They know what to
do, but they don't like it."

"Good," Aidan said as he climbed on the back of
the alpha male.

The opposing mek took a step forward. "Surrender.
We have you outnumbered and we have your two other
coterie members held hostage. If you attack, we will kill
them along with you."

Aidan caught a glimpse of Palomas and Fig, hiding
on opposite sides just outside the cave entrance. Fig
struggled to hold a single mechanical arm from his
damaged suit. He aimed it at the top of the cave entrance
and nodded. Palomas gave a single nod. It was time.

"You ready?" Aidan asked Masay.

"Let's get this over with," Masay responded.

Aidan kicked the wolfstag and they rushed toward the enemy. The mek took aim to fire a volley of rockets from his wrists, but before they released, Masay sped to the mek, pushing the mek's arms upward just enough to send the rockets firing into the empty sky above their heads. Aidan and the wolfstags attacked, pushing the entire enemy coterie back into the cavern and pinning them inside.

"NOW!" Aidan shouted.

Fig pushed a button, sending a single rocket from his mek suit arm into the top of the cave entrance. The rocket's aim was true, and it exploded in a fiery ball of destruction. On the other side of the entrance, Palomas beat the outside of the cavern with her powerful fists of fury. The cavern quaked, trembling from Fig's rocket and Palomas' repetitive blows. Before the opposing coterie realized what was happening, the cavern collapsed in a heap of heavy rocks and snow, crushing them, Masay, and Aidan.

Everyone but Fig and Palomas had been eliminated, leaving them alive to claim the victory for their coterie.

WOLFSTAG

CHAPTER 10: TRUST

I remember the day the second Splicer War began. The creatures spread like wildfire through the streets of Hashmeer, cutting down men, women and children like trees in a forest. My heart nearly broke when I learned the cause. My colleague and my friend, Doctor Panoa Hashmeer, had brought the very plague upon us we believed we had escaped when we left our beloved home of Justus.

—Doctor T.M. Omori,
Man's Quest for Destruction: A Case for the Prime Initiative

I wish my parents could have seen the trial today," Fig said between bites of his sweet cake.

In celebration of their win, Aidan invited the whole coterie to hang out in his room after the curfew bell sounded. Setting the security cameras on a loop, they snuck over to the commissary and printed out dozens of sweet cakes and power drinks for a night of relaxation.

"You know," Fig continued with his mouth half full, "I wonder if they would be proud of me, now that I'm a mek? Maybe they'd hate me for it. Or maybe they'd praise me for going to fight in the war. I wonder if they miss me? Do they even remember me?"

Fig tended to turn thoughtful and nostalgic when he stayed up late. This was a conversation he, Aidan and Palomas had mulled over dozens of times. *What were their parents like? Did they have real blood brothers and sisters? Did their families miss them? Would they ever see them again?*

Masay swallowed the rest of his sweet cake and grabbed another one. Aidan noticed that Masay had downed at least twelve sweet cakes, and the red vigori showed no signs of slowing down.

"They probably think you're dead," Masay said bluntly before scarfing down another cake. "And if they saw your little blue behind they'd want nothing to do with you. You're a freak, a prime, and they're human."

Palomas threw a pillow at Masay, hitting him square in the face. "MASAY! That was totally rude!" Palomas signed angrily.

Masay shrugged his shoulders and grabbed another sweet cake. "Sorry," he said, crumbs falling from his lips. "It's just the truth."

"But don't you want to see your parents? Don't you want to know where you came from?" Fig asked.

Masay paused for a moment before answering. "No. I am what I am and there's no going back. The Director took away my blood family and my coterie. For that I will always hate him. If anything, I wish I could join the rebellion."

"The rebellion?" Aidan asked.

Masay raised an eyebrow and downed the cake in his hand. "Man, you guys are sheltered at Mount Fegorio. There's an underground rebellion of primes and humans working together to overthrow the Director. Word is the Director's been trying to stop them, but they are too quick and he can never find them. Anyone who can stand up to the Director is a winner in my book."

Fig and Palomas looked intrigued at the idea of a rebellion, while Masay licked his sticky fingers clean.

"What about you?" Masay asked Aidan. "You've been quiet. Are you homesick for your mama and dada too?"

Aidan's eyes smiled at the thought of his parents. He didn't feel particularly homesick for them, as Masay teased, but someday he planned to find out who they were when he graduated from Mount Fegorio. If he could control puzzler mode, he should be able to hack his way into any of the Ethos Army databases and find out who his parents were. There was only so much information he could access from Mount Fegorio.

"I would like nothing more than to meet my parents," Aidan answered. "Someday I'll find them, but that someday won't be for a long time. I just have to be patient."

"Maybe you should join the rebellion," Masay said. "I bet they could help you."

Aidan laughed at the comment. "Right. And maybe Fig will wake up an eidetic and be ten feet tall."

"Hey, anything's possible," Fig protested, placing his stool on top of Aidan's desk and climbing to the top.

"Look at me. My name is General Estrago," he said in a perfect General Estrago voice. He mimicked pulling at an invisible beard and cracked his neck. "I have memorized every book in the world. I'm stiffer than a dead body that's been petrified and then frozen, and it's impossible for me to take or tell a joke. I'm as tall as six meks, and I seriously have the hots for Captain Solsti."

Aidan and Palomas laughed at the dead-on impression, though no sound came from Palomas as she smiled and her shoulders moved up and down. But Masay lost control, falling out of his chair and doubling over in laughter.

"That...was...perfect," he said between breaths. "Oh man, I haven't laughed that hard in years."

"Thank you, thank you," Fig said with a bow.

After a few more minutes the laughter wore off, replaced by a series of slow yawns from everyone in the room but Aidan.

"Well, I think I'm ready for bed," Palomas signed. "Good night, losers. I love you."

"Love you too," Aidan and Fig answered automatically. Masay said nothing, looking awkwardly at the ground during the exchange.

Palomas threw another pillow at Masay, getting his attention. "Masay. That means you too. Good night, loser. I love you."

"Uhmm…I love…you too," he offered clumsily.

Palomas simply nodded her approval and exited the room.

Masay arched an eyebrow and looked at Aidan and Fig. They both smiled at him.

"Palomas approves," Aidan said. "I guess that means you're one of us now, brother."

***

"Do you want to explain to me what we're doing?" Masay asked. His fiery red hair bobbed up and down as he helped Palomas unbolt two of the trainer seats from the senior boys' dormitory.

Palomas did not answer.

Dixon and Zana had given her the password to their senior dorm room and made sure it would be empty during dinner while Palomas and Masay worked to remove the seats.

"Don't get me wrong. I like pulling a prank on the seniors as much as the next prime, but I usually like to know why I'm doing things."

Palomas continued to ignore the boy. She was still upset with him for making her late to their lug training course that afternoon. Because there were no vigori instructors at Mount Fegorio—or any other complex—Masay was assigned to attend the lug training course for the year.

Masay and Palomas had planned to meet at the commissary so they could go to the class together. She arrived first and waited five minutes for him, but he didn't show. Concerned, she went to his room, Aidan's room, his previous class, and still no sign of Masay. Realizing she was late, she began jogging down the main hallway toward the gymnasium, which was a half mile on the other side of the second level ring. A red blur sped through the hallway and slowed down at her side.

"Where have you been?" she asked. "I was worried."

"Sorry, I had to meet with General Estrago and got lost finding my way back."

"How could you get lost?" Palomas questioned. "The levels are just giant circles that go around and around."

"I know," Masay answered. "I've been doing laps trying to find the gymnasium. I must keep missing it."

Palomas shook her head, annoyed. She dreaded finding out what her punishment would be for being late to class. Last time she was late, Captain Blakey made her spend the entire class carrying a 500-pound lift ball back and forth across the gymnasium. It was one of the few times in her life that her muscles had actually ached.

Palomas and Masay jogged up to a larger-than-normal sliding door in the hallway. It had a large holovid sign above it that read, "Gymnasium."

"Yeah, I can see how you missed this big door with the big sign," she signed to Masay, shaking her head in annoyance.

Masay only shrugged and put his arm forward for her to pass. "After you," he said with a smile.

The gymnasium was stationed on the opposite side of the second-level ring from the assembly hall. It matched the assembly hall in size, spanning the first, second and third levels of the complex. Exercise equipment, massive weights, and various weapons were stationed around the walls of the spacious gymnasium, while the open center of the room was lined with padded mats for combat training.

The rest of the lugs stood in a straight line at attention while Captain Blakey signed instructions. Palomas and Masay rushed down the steps from the second-level entrance to the bottom floor of the gymnasium. Their footsteps echoed across the large expanse, catching Captain Blakey's attention along with the rest of the class.

"You're late!" signed Captain Blakey, the lug master instructor. The man stood just over six feet tall, with his golden hair in a short flat-top and muscles attempting to bulge loose from the much-too-small, gold-colored workout clothes he wore. A single gold whistle hung from his thick neck, and he eyed Masay with a dubious look of curiosity.

Reaching the rest of the class, Palomas and Masay lined up and saluted.

"Sorry for being late, sir," Masay quickly responded.

"A vigori," Captain Blakey signed. "I haven't seen a vigori in years. Not since I had my arm nearly ripped off by a Splicer on the front at Omori."

Captain Blakey rubbed his left shoulder, staring off into the distance for a moment.

"I thought vigori were supposed to be fast. What in Ethos caused you to be late on your first day of class?"

Palomas' shoulders slumped ever so slightly as she stood at attention. Masay had an excuse. He had been with General Estrago. She, on the other hand, had no valid excuse. Telling Captain Blakey she was late because she was waiting to come to class with Masay would only bring the ridicule of the captain. He already thought of her as a second-class lug simply because she was a girl. In fact, she was the only girl lug in the whole complex. Very few females became lugs after their infant injection.

Masay continued to stand at attention, but did not answer.

"Well," demanded Captain Blakey. "If you two have no excuse, I have a lovely 500-pound lift ball with both your names on it. I'd expect such wimpy, womanly behavior from Palomas, but not from a vigori."

Masay glanced at Palomas from the corner of his eye and frowned. "Permission to speak freely, sir."

Captain Blakey nodded.

"We were late because I was waiting for Palomas to show me to class. She was busy washing her hair and then got lost bringing us here. Girls! Am I right?"

The other lugs in line let out breathy laughs, all except the senior lug named Wesley. A smug smile twitched at the corners of Captain Blakey's mouth as he looked at Palomas and her golden hair that was pulled up in a tight bun.

Palomas' ears and cheeks burned a deeper shade of gold, almost brown, and her eyes bore a look of death into the side of Masay's skull.

Captain Blakey huffed. "Fine. I'm feeling generous today since you're new. Both of you get in line. We're practicing grappling techniques today. I hope you can keep up," he said to Masay.

Palomas felt a little better as she ruthlessly pinned nearly every boy to the mat. The only two exceptions were Wesley, who pinned her in a surprise move she had never seen before, and Masay. Every time she grabbed an arm or leg, Masay would vibrate himself loose before her grip could tighten.

"Listen, if you're still upset about the class, I'm sorry," Masay conceded back in the senior dormitory. "Like I said a hundred times before, I only said those things to get us out of being punished. It worked, didn't it?"

Palomas continued unbolting the trainer seat, offering no response.

"Or are you mad because you couldn't pin me? Don't feel bad. Vigori are slippery creatures. Plus, I didn't pin you. You were way too strong. Consider it a tie."

Palomas showed no sign of acknowledgement as she worked away in silence.

Masay moved his arms in rapid speed, quickly unbolting the trainer seat in front of him and unharnessing the cables connected to the seat.

"Fine. You don't need to talk to me," he said calmly, his voice a step lower than normal. "I'm used to silence. I've been alone for the past six months since the last of my coterie died at the Ice Mount complex."

Palomas stopped working and lifted her head toward Masay. Thoughts of her own diminished coterie racked her mind. She was only twelve, and already she had lost nine of her coterie. She vowed she would lose no one else.

"What happened to them?" she signed. Her serious golden eyes locked with Masay, who held her stare with deep burning eyes that betrayed his youth. There was a pain there she recognized in her own past.

"Half our coterie died in infancy," Masay said. "*A bad batch*, the masters told us. Of the six remaining, Lelani and Simbo were puzzlers who died from the shakes around age two, just after they learned to walk. Mason was a huge eidetic, ten feet tall at age ten. He had a heart attack in his sleep. And the last two. They…"

Masay turned his head to the side, fighting back tears that were welling up in his eyes. He appeared self-conscious of his emotions, and Palomas' heart began to soften towards the boy. She moved to sit next to him.

"Go on," she signed. "It's good to talk about what happened to them. I know. Aidan, Fig and I are the only three left from our original twelve."

Masay wiped his eyes in an attempt to hide the tears trickling down his red cheek.

"We were on a training exercise out on the slopes of the Ice Mount. Our complex was much like this, but the mountain was covered in snow with a thick glacier of ice underneath."

"You were allowed outside the complex? On the side of the mountain?" Palomas questioned.

Masay nodded, "Yeah. We went out there all the time for training exercises and cold weather combat. Why? Don't you ever leave the complex?"

Palomas shook her head. She had never seen the outside of Mount Fegorio.

Masay raised a puzzled eyebrow, but she prodded him to continue.

"My sister Junis, an agulator, and my brother Gazeem, a vibrunt, were all that was left of our coterie. We were finishing a patrol exercise when the ground shook from a mild earthquake. It lasted only a few seconds and everything seemed fine. The masters immediately called us back to the complex and ended the exercise. We were nearly to the complex when a stampeding flock of walguins slid down the mountain toward us. The walguins were huge—the size of bearcats—and we barely dodged out of their way as they rushed past us down the mountain. The mountain rumbled a second time and we were not ready for what came next. We realized too late why the walguins had stampeded past us when a massive wall of ice and snow came barreling toward us.

"We tried to outrun it, sliding down the mountain on our skis as quickly as possible, but it was no use. Within seconds we were beaten, tossed, and buried by the avalanche. It felt like a gang of lugs had used me as a punching bag. I was knocked unconscious and when I came to, I was buried in snow. I called out to my brother and sister, but they were gone."

Following her maternal instincts, Palomas put her arm around Masay. She was tough as cortunium nails and could hold a grudge like no one else, but right now Masay needed her. She loved and protected her coterie like a mother bearcat, and Masay was part of her coterie now.

Masay allowed Palomas to embrace him as the floodgates opened, and he sobbed like a newly-injected infant. Eventually, he regained his composure, wiping away his tears and smoothing back his bright red hair, which immediately stood straight back in the air like a flame.

"I was able to escape by using my powers, vibrating quickly and digging a hole to the surface. I searched and searched for them, but I couldn't find the others. Eventually a search party from the Ice Mount reached me and dragged me back to the complex. It took them another week, but they finally found Junis' and Gazeem's frozen bodies. I've been alone ever since."

Palomas gently patted him on the back. "It's okay," she signed. "You have a new coterie now. A new family."

Masay nodded gratefully. "Thank you. That really does mean a lot. Oh, and if you could do me a favor and not tell the guys about me crying like this, I would appreciate it."

Typical boy, Palomas thought, but she smiled and nodded.

"Can I tell you one more thing?" Masay tentatively asked.

Palomas nodded reassuringly.

He stopped speaking out loud and switched to sign language. "I *hate* the masters. I *hate* what they force us to do, and I especially *hate* the Director. Our brothers and sisters die every day, and it's all their fault. They don't care about us. We're just tools to them, bred to fight a war we know nothing about. As soon as I can manage, I'm going to escape. I'm going to join the rebellion."

WALGUIN

CHAPTER 11: FEELINGS

I am writing my argument for the Prime Initiative in the old ways of paper binding, in addition to electronic means. I do this for one reason—so that it might survive. If nothing else, this is a history of our people and a reminder of the mistakes we made that brought about our destruction with the Splicer War.

I fear that if I only publish this electronically, it may one day be rooted out and deleted forever by my growing list of foes. Hashmeer is already lost and the ruling politicians of Omori and Ethos waste time bickering back and forth. They are too young to remember the horrors of the Splicer plague on Justus and they waver with indecision, accomplishing nothing.

They fear the power of the primes, when they should fear the Splicers more—much more. But I have not forgotten what happened on Justus. If they do not approve the Prime Initiative soon, all will be lost.

—Doctor T.M. Omori,

Man's Quest for Destruction: A Case for the Prime Initiative

Aidan sat at his desk, flipping open the weathered green cover of *Man's Quest for Destruction: A Case for the Prime Initiative*. It was late, everyone was asleep, and he grew tired of working on his new tech to use in Sim 299.

Questions plagued his mind and he wanted answers. He thirsted to know more about the origins of his ancestors from Justus, the origins of the Splicers, the origins of the Director, and especially his own origins.

Who are my parents? What are they like? Do they know I'm alive? Do they miss me?

He thumbed through the pages of the bound book and sighed.

"I can't get answers about my parents right now," he said to himself. "But I might find some other answers in this old book."

The reading was tedious, to say the least. The first sixty pages contained a depressingly long-winded prologue by the author, Doctor T.M. Omori. In the lengthy opening, Doctor Omori ranted on the weakness of mankind and the natural failings of humanity. He loathed the corruption and incompetence of the current political systems in both Ethos and Omori, and especially his own lack of authority to move forward and take action with the Prime Initiative.

Lastly, he mourned the loss of Hashmeer and the return of the Splicers. It was here that Aidan's perseverance paid off.

We came to the Univi star system to escape the Splicers. I still remember our old home world of Justus. I was a mere teenager, only eighteen, when we escaped. Because of my youth and my gifted scientific prowess, I was chosen by the leaders of Justus as one of the 13,000 passengers allowed to board the ARCs. The Splicers ravaged our world and it was only a matter of time before our forces would be overrun. We entered the experimental starship, leaving behind hundreds of thousands of our people to be destroyed by the Splicers.

But, we would survive—humanity's new hope. We knew we were taking a one-way trip to the furthest hospitable star system in our databases, the Univi system. Only recently discovered, the Univi system held three planets within the hospitable zone from its sun. Normally, an exploration journey of this distance would take three lifetimes to reach Univi from Justus, but the experimental propulsion of the ARCs would last long enough for us to reach the Univi system in a much-shortened three-year period.

It's been eighty-six years since we first arrived in the Univi system. I am an old man now, and I have seen much in my time. I've seen our worlds flourish and our populations grow one hundred fold over these last five generations. The horrors of Justus became a distant memory and a folktale we told our children at night to scare them into obedience.

That is, until we discovered that my colleague and former friend, Doctor Panoa Hashmeer, had betrayed us all and brought the Splicers to the Univi system.

Aidan quickly turned the page to continue reading. He was engrossed by Doctor Omori's historic account, but dismayed by what he saw on the next page. It read:

CHAPTER ONE: The Beginnings of the Primes

The never-ending prologue appeared to have ended, and with it ended the information about Doctor Panoa Hashmeer and the origin of the Splicers to the Univi system.

Aidan turned more pages, searching for any sign of the name Doctor Panoa Hashmeer. He wished he could read the book on his quire, knowing that a simple text search would pull up everything available on Doctor Hashmeer in seconds.

Soon he found himself shouting at the book. "How did Doctor Hashmeer betray them?! How did she bring the Splicers here?!"

But the book did not answer.

Aidan continued to flip through random pages scanning for more information about Doctor Hashmeer, but his search was cut short by the morning bell.

I can't believe it's already morning, he thought, looking at the time on his quire processor. His stomach twisted and turned as the importance of the day dawned on him. Thoughts of Doctor Hashmeer and Doctor Omori dissipated into the recesses of his mind.

This is the day, he thought. *We go back into Sim 299 tonight.*

***

General Estrago and Captain Solsti sat side by side in the laboratory, each looking at their own sets of blood samples from various prime cadets. General Estrago used a light spectrometer and longview magnifier with the results displayed on his holovid.

Holovid projections were not clearly visible to Captain Solsti's vibruntcy, but she used her own methods to study the samples. During her time as a doctor on the front lines of Omori, she had developed her senses to not only push away and see the landscape surrounding her, but also to pull inward on specific objects, seeing them on a microscopic level. This allowed her to see and diagnose internal injuries in both prime and human soldiers. She could also diagnose most illnesses, but those were only seen in humans, since primes never became ill.

To use this skill of microscopic vibruntcy required extreme focus on her part, which at the moment proved difficult to maintain with General Estrago sitting mere inches away.

Her heart raced as she looked up from her work to see the scarred, brown face of the general. Although she was considered tall by most, standing just over six feet, her slender green body was dwarfed by the ten-foot eidetic. She traced the scars on his face with her vibrunt vision, watching them run from his forehead, over his cheeks, and down his neck, and then disappear below the high collar of his brown uniform.

She often wondered how he received such brutal scars. Presumably they came from his time serving on Omori. She knew he had been a doctor, scientist, and decorated battle tactician on the warfront, but as an eidetic he would have been kept off the front lines. Whenever she asked how he received the scars, General Estrago simply changed the subject.

Some of the staff and other masters at Mount Fegorio found General Estrago's scars grotesque and his size overbearing, but Captain Solsti admired them, as she did General Estrago's abilities. He was calm, grounded, and more knowledgeable than any person she had ever met, and he was strong—strong in mind and in body. She admired his fairness as a leader, his loyalty to his troops and his desire to do good...and because of this, she loved him.

She knew their feelings could never be acted upon. They had discussed the matter at length and in secret, both sharing their mutual affections. Although she had been thrilled beyond belief to know he felt the same for her, his firmness for the rules left her dejected, questioning her self-worth. He refused to act upon their feelings and made her swear to do the same.

"I care about you too much for us to jeopardize your life or have you sent away," he had said. "If the only piece of hidden joy I have each day is seeing you, then that is enough. It must be enough."

She had cried at this response, and he'd wrapped his large arms around her, holding her tight in comfort. His warmth and touch sent a shockwave through her body. It was the last time he had touched her in two years.

But what if it's not enough for me? she thought, looking at the man as he focused intently at his work beside her. She daydreamed of running away with him to the rebellion. The rebellion was growing each day, miraculously avoiding the hunters of Director Tuskin. If only he would agree to join the rebellion. Then they could escape and be together.

But she knew he would never do so. His loyalty to his command, to the war effort, and especially to the cadets, was unwavering.

Still, after two years since he last held her close, her heart raced.

"You've been staring at me for three minutes and thirty-three seconds," said General Estrago, without taking his focus away from his work. "Is something amiss with my hair? Do I have a baby spidergoose crawling in it?"

Captain Solsti shook her head and chuckled. "No, General. Nothing of the sort is wrong. I was only lost in thought. Daydreaming, really, although it is night so I suppose I was night-dreaming."

General Estrago turned away from his work, looking down into her rich, green eyes. Although she was blind, her eyes captivated him every time he saw her. "Well, I hope it was a pleasant *night-dream*," he said.

"It was the best kind," she replied. She smiled, but her eyes betrayed the sadness behind them.

"Perhaps you should retire for the evening. It is quite late, and we have been researching for hours with little to show for our efforts."

Captain Solsti nodded. She was tired, but she did not want to leave his side.

"So you've not found anything new in the defect mutations either?" she asked rhetorically. "Perhaps the quire processor test results have always been correct."

General Estrago sighed and pulled at his beard. She found the mannerism endearing.

"These tests are run each year on the mainframe quire processors. They search for the link to the defects of the primes, but nothing is ever found. That to me is impossible. They are missing something. Some calculation is wrong. With billions of sequences, it will take more than my lifetime to search them all on my own."

"That's why I'm here to help you," Captain Solsti said and smiled.

General Estrago released another sigh and his own countenance softened. "I can't explain it, but I know there is an answer somewhere in these sequences, and for some reason I feel compelled to find it."

"You will," Captain Solsti said, reaching out her hand instinctively before she realized what she was doing. She placed her hand on top of his and gently squeezed. A tingling shock coursed through her body, similar to the way she felt two years ago as he held her tight. General Estrago did not pull his hand away. She felt magnetized to him, not wanting to let go. Their eyes remained fixed on one another, and General Estrago's breaths came more quickly, while her heart seemed to jump from her chest.

"To Hashmeer with it," he said, pulling her in for a passionate kiss. But only seconds into the sweet sensation of their lips touching, he abruptly pushed her away.

"What have I done?" he whispered. "I'm sorry…I must go. I should never have…" His voice trailed off as he rapidly exited the laboratory, leaving Captain Solsti standing alone, holding a hand to her lips.

BATMONKEY

CHAPTER 12: UPGRADES

Seven classes of primes have been discovered thus far: Agulators, Lugs, Eidetics, Puzzlers, Vibrunts, Vigori and Readers. It's been debated which class of prime is the most powerful. I find the argument moot, for it is the Splicers that are still the most powerful. In every way, they are the combination of all prime powers.

—Doctor T.M. Omori,
Man's Quest for Destruction: A Case for the Prime Initiative

General Estrago stomped into his room and gripped both sides of his wash basin. He filled it up with cold water and dunked his head beneath the surface, letting the icy sensation clear his mind. He opened his eyes under the water and looked at the metal surface of the basin, admiring the clean and simple surface.

Pulling his head out of the water, he took a large breath.

"Clean and simple," he muttered to himself. "Why couldn't I just keep things clean and simple?"

He looked at himself in the mirror, water dripping down his hideously scarred face. He couldn't believe he had kissed her. If anyone found out, life would get messy.

Still, the kiss had been amazing. The more his mind lingered on the kiss, the more he wondered what Solsti could possibly see in him and his ugly, broken face.

"I guess I have a face that only a blind woman could love," he joked to himself.

He walked back out to his main quarters and sat down at his desk, collecting his thoughts. Suddenly, his quire beeped and an image of Director Tuskin's head appeared on the holovid in his room.

"Hello, General," Director Tuskin said coldly. "I'm glad to see I did not wake you. Are you okay? You look…rather wet."

General Estrago bowed his head. "I'm fine, sir. How may I be of assistance?"

"There are things in motion that require your help to achieve," Director Tuskin said. "Here is the role I have laid out for you."

General Estrago listened, his eyes widening ever further as Director Tuskin explained his plan in detail.

"You want me to do what?!" General Estrago asked incredulously, shaking his head in confusion.

"You heard me correctly, Estrago. Follow my directions precisely and we will kill three cobramoths with one stone. Do you understand?"

The man has finally gone mad, General Estrago thought. *This makes no sense.*

"General Estrago!" The Director bellowed. "If you're not capable of such a simple task, I may have to enforce my rule of non-fraternization between you and Captain Solsti. Do you understand?"

No, not Solsti, General Estrago thought. *How did the Director know so quickly? If the Director enforced his rule, Solsti could be executed.*

If it were only his life in jeopardy, he would defy the Director the same way he and his coterie had defied the tyrant as young teenage primes. He knew he was dying and did not care about himself, but he could not risk Solsti's life. He loved the green vibrunt woman with his heart and soul. He would see that no harm came to her.

"Estrago," the Director repeated. "Do you understand?"

"Yes," General Estrago said, bowing his head. "I will obey."

***

Zana and Fig traded ideas and insults like long-lost friends recently reunited after years apart. Aidan found it amusing to observe them working together. They drooled over one another's mek suits and tech creations, hoping to glean as much information as possible. Fig would suggest improvements to Zana's suit, which Zana ridiculed and praised in the same breath, but then quickly implemented. Zana gave Fig suggestions to enhance his gadgets, which Fig laughed to scorn and then hurriedly typed down in his quire processor so he wouldn't forget them.

The whole scene was amazing to Aidan, considering meks were infamous for their greedy and secretive nature when it came to tech. Even amongst their own coteries, a mek would rarely, if ever, share their tech. Aidan did not know why, but all meks appeared to be wired this way. But watching Zana and Fig work side by side gave him hope. It was the first time he had ever seen two meks actually work together and enjoy it.

The four of them—Aidan, Dixon, Zana and Fig— had worked feverishly the past week to build upgrades they could use in Sim 299. As Zana pointed out after their first encounter in the sim, "We *all* need upgrades if we're going to survive."

That meant Dixon and Aidan needed to build their own tech, under the guidance of Zana and Fig. The rules of the Pit simulations would only let them use tech that they had created and built themselves, according to the first rule of mek technology. Few primes, other than meks, went to any lengths to build their own tech. They preferred to use their natural abilities. But the four of them understood that their natural abilities would not be enough for Sim 299.

It was only hours before their scheduled reentry into the simulation, and Aidan felt the nervousness he had pushed down begin to swell in his stomach. This was new territory for him in Sim 299. He had no idea what they were going to face, and he wondered what lay at the end of the sim.

The dinner bell rang, but all four of them continued working. This in and of itself was a miracle for Fig, but the lust of creating new tech eased his hunger pains. Since Fig and Palomas had gleaned information about Sim 299 via Fig's vibrunt ears, Aidan had enlisted Fig's help as a tech consultant. Although Fig did not actually build anything with his own hands, he and Zana provided Aidan and Dixon with detailed plans, instructions, and oversight as they built their personal upgrades. They put the finishing touches on their new tech with only an hour to spare.

"I hope these work," Dixon said, picking up his creation.

"If they don't work, it's your own fault," Fig chided. "You're the ones who built them. Don't blame the genius architects for your poor construction."

Zana gave Fig a fist bump. "Truer words have never been spoken."

Dixon threw an empty drink bottle at Fig from across the room. "It will always be your fault," Dixon teased.

Aidan sat at his desk against the wall and lifted the pocket-sized tube of cortunium metal he had worked on all week. It had yet to be tested, which worried him. He gripped the metal tube and flicked the first switch on the side. A sword of blue flames erupted from one end of the tube. He flicked the second switch on the handle, and an ice blade formed out the other side of the tube.

"Tuskin's fury!" Fig and Zana swore in unison.

"Be careful with that," Zana scolded.

"Yeah," Fig continued. "This isn't the Pit. That flame can cut through nearly anything—that's why it needed the cortunium casing. Plus, one touch of the ice blade will cause permanent frostbite."

"Well, theoretically that's what it can do," Zana corrected. "But I don't want to find out in real life."

Dixon looked at the sword approvingly. "At least, *theoretically*, we know it works before we try to use it in the sim." He took his own creation, a new hooded cloak, and wrapped it around himself, pulling the hood over his face. He pushed a sensor attached to the inside of the cloak, and immediately his whole form turned invisible.

Aidan, Zana and Fig stared in amazement.

"Is it working?" Dixon asked, his voice coming from the chair he sat in, which appeared empty.

"Uhmm, yeah. It's working and I'm a mad super genius!" Zana cheered.

"Try to move around," Fig suggested.

Dixon took a few steps around the room and a translucent image flitted in and out of view as he moved.

"Hmm, it's not perfect," Zana said. "But it's still pretty awesome!"

The cloak had been created using pinhole-size cameras doubling as holovid projectors. The first time Zana and Dixon came to Aidan's room, Aidan showed them the hidden pinhole cameras in his walls. Fascinated, Zana replicated the camera and helped Dixon to print them into the fabric of a new cloak. The cameras worked simultaneously to record images from one side and project the image on the opposite side, causing the wearer to appear invisible.

"And what about you?" Aidan asked. "Will the upgrades to your suit work?"

Zana nodded confidently. "Yeah. I got this."

After her fight with the human warrior, Zana decided she needed more than one set of arms in case the first ones were ripped off again. Now her suit was lined with three arms protruding from each side instead of one. Each arm was independently controlled using a modified control system that Fig had helped design. In addition to the new arms, she strengthened the armor with a diamond-coated polymer and used Fig's expertise to add a 'Lug Mode' switch to her own suit.

"Just so you know," Fig said, "I'm copying all of those upgrades to my own suit."

Zana nodded approvingly. "Fair enough, but you've got to show me how to make my own vibrunt ears."

"Deal," Fig agreed, and the two shook on it.

Someone pounded on the outside of the door and Aidan used his quire to connect to the cameras in the hallway. "It's Palomas and Masay."

"Perfect. I'll get the door," Dixon offered with a chuckle. He was still hiding under in his invisibility cloak.

The door slid open, and Palomas walked in carrying a trainer seat in each hand. She showed no sign of strain as she hefted the massive metal chairs into the room. Masay followed close behind carrying a box filled with the bolts and connection cables required to set up the chairs.

Aidan had rigged the cameras to hide the two as they smuggled the trainer seats through the complex while everyone was at dinner in the commissary. Aidan, Dixon, and Zana wanted to enter the sim together from the same room to avoid interruptions. This also allowed Fig, Palomas, and Masay to keep an eye on them in case something went wrong.

The only hiccup with their plan was that they needed Dixon's and Zana's personal seats from their dormitory to make this work. Each personal seat was programmed to only let the specific user log into the sims from their seat. Luckily, they had a lug in their group who could carry them a quarter mile without breaking a sweat.

"Did anyone see you?" Aidan asked.

Masay shook his head. "We had a couple close calls, but I kept racing back and forth to make sure no one saw us."

Palomas gently set the chairs into place. "Where is Dixon?" she signed.

"Boo!" Dixon whispered in Masay's ear and grabbed him by the shoulder from behind. Masay took off running at an inhuman speed across the room.

"What's wrong with you?" Palomas signed.

Masay looked infuriated. "Where are you?" he seethed to the empty space around him. "I know that was you, Dixon. How are you hiding yourself?"

"You'll never find me," Dixon teased, his voice coming from behind Palomas this time, causing her to jump.

"How is that possible?" she signed to Aidan.

Aidan smiled. "Invisibility cloak. Pretty cool, huh?"

"He won't be invisible for long," Masay shouted. He dashed around the room at dizzying speeds, reaching his arms out in hopes of finding the invisible form of Dixon.

With his vigori powers near top speed, Masay was a blur of red around the room. It was said that a trained vigori could outpace a bipod racer at 300 mph and their body would never tire from the exertion, so long as they had constant nourishment. Food was their defect. The more energy they used, the more they needed to eat, and if they didn't eat at least every twelve hours, they died.

"Uh, uh, uh—won't find me there," Dixon taunted from above their heads.

"Of course, you're floating," Masay hissed. "But not for long."

Sending a burst of speed through his body, he ran up the side of the wall, onto the ceiling, and jumped directly to the spot where Dixon's voice was last heard.

THUD.

Before Dixon could react, Masay crashed down into him, tackling Dixon to the floor below. Acting from years of training, Dixon instinctively changed his weight to a boulder, protecting himself from injury as he hit the hard steel floor with the incredible force of Masay's speed.

Masay was not so lucky. His right arm produced an unnatural crack as he hit the floor, the bottom half of his arm bending sideways. His head slammed into the floor next, leaving a deep gash across his forehead. Bright red blood flowed from the gash and dribbled to the floor.

"Holy hippophants!" Fig swore, paling at the sight of Masay's disfigured arm and bloody head.

Palomas rushed to Masay's side. "Are you okay?" she signed.

"I'm fine," Masay grunted. He dug into his pocket with his good arm and pulled out a compact square, tossing it into his mouth and swallowing it whole. "10,000 calorie energy bar," he said through gritted teeth. He grabbed his right arm and twisted it back into place at the elbow. The bones and sinews in his forearm made a sickening crunching noise as he pushed it back into place.

The gash on his head rapidly knitted itself together, and the blood flow stopped. He let out a sigh of relief, and tested his right arm, bending it back and forth. "There, all better," he announced.

"Hey, what about me?" Dixon complained, sitting up from the floor. The cloak had slid off his lower body, exposing his legs while leaving his torso and head invisible.

"Now that's just weird looking," Zana said, taking a picture of the half-bodied Dixon with her quire processor.

Palomas lifted Dixon up in the air, pulled his cloak off, and tossed him onto the bed. "You got what you deserved," she signed.

"Hey, careful with the cloak," Dixon protested, quickly taking it back from Palomas. "You have to admit though, it's pretty cool, right?"

"Not as cool as Masay running up the wall," Fig said, still amazed. "And then his head and arm just healed in seconds. Leaping lemurtoads, Masay! I mean, c'mon, your arm was bent this way and you just put it back in place. Am I the only one who saw that happen?"

None of them had ever seen a vigori heal themselves. Apparently the rumors were true. Not only were vigori impossibly fast, but they healed incredibly quickly when given enough nourishment. That's why they were commonly agreed upon as the most capable warriors among all the varieties of primes. It took a lot to take down a vigori for good.

"Yeah, I guess it was kind of cool," Dixon relented, annoyed they were ignoring his invisible cloak. "But that didn't mean the runt had to tackle me out of the air."

"Anyways," Aidan interjected, trying to prevent another argument and possible fight from breaking out, "we've still got work to do. Let's get these trainer seats connected and ready to launch us into the sim. It's going to be a long night."

To Aidan's mild surprise, the bickering stopped and everyone went to work. He still found it unnerving that they all followed his orders as if he were a general.

Within thirty minutes, all three trainer seats were connected, and Aidan, Dixon, and Zana took their places.

"So, is anyone going to tell me what's going on yet?" Masay asked. "I've gathered you're secretly going into a sim with two seniors, which makes no sense, and that you need us here to stand watch."

Everyone looked to Aidan for a response.

Palomas fully trusted Masay, and Aidan was thankful for his help in the trial, but he still wasn't sure if they could share more information without incurring the wrath of Sentinel. Plus, a part of him still wondered at the timing of Masay's arrival.

"We can't share any more information with you. At least not yet," Aidan replied. "But thank you for your help today. We will explain everything when this is finished."

Aidan turned to Palomas and Fig. "Be ready for us. When and if we die in the sim, we should awaken and be able to return back to it. I'm guessing it's going to be a long night, so we will need water and snacks ready to keep up our strength before reentering. Everyone understand?"

They all nodded, except Masay.

"Okay. Let's do this."

Aidan, Dixon, and Zana secured their headbands and connected their quires to their seats.

"Ready for connection to the Pit," a female computerized voice read. "Entry to simulation 299 in 5-4-3-2-1."

Aidan's mind jolted into a tailspin. Blurred images flashed all around him in wild succession. He knew none of this was real, but the spinning seemed to pull at every fiber of his body. He tried to focus on the images as they passed, but only caught glimpses of doctors in white coats. It looked like a Splicer laid on a table, but he couldn't be sure. The images spun faster and faster and a wave of nausea hit him like he'd been punched in the gut. The image of the white cosmic cloud came into view, but this time the dark matter seemed to be devouring the bright cloud as the light disappeared. Suddenly, all went black. Three glowing eyes stared at him from the darkness. He blinked and the darkness was replaced by the courtyard of the castle. Dixon stood to his right and Zana to his left.

"Well, that's a plus," Zana said, looking around the courtyard. "At least we don't have to cross the acid moat and face those psycho statues again."

Aidan and Dixon nodded in agreement.

All three of them turned their gaze to the sky as a large shadow passed overhead. The trio watched the regal form of Sentinel, the dragleon, land gracefully before them. His golden mane blew gently in the breeze, and the blood-red scales of his body shone brightly in the sun.

"Hello again, young primes. I see you have kept your oaths of secrecy?"

The three nodded in affirmation.

Sentinel growled. "But only barely. I know about your friends, young Aidan. They are quite resourceful. But you kept your oaths, and the three of you may enter your next challenge. If you so desire, Aidan, you may share with your coterie what you experience this night, but no others may know."

Sentinel stared at Dixon. The senior wished he could share everything with Kara and tell her the truth. But he nodded in acknowledgment of Sentinel's orders.

The dragleon shifted his gaze toward the horizon. He appeared distant and distracted. The courtyard air hung in awkward silence as they waited for Sentinel to continue his explanation of the imminent challenge, but none came.

Impatient, Zana raised all three of the right hands on her suit. "Uhm, yeah, about that, Master Sentinel. I have a question."

The dragleon pulled his attention back to the trio. "Yes, what is your question young Zana?"

Zana put her three arms down. "Pretend we don't know what the second challenge is, or anything about this crazy place. How would you explain what we are supposed to do next, and do you have any tips to beat the challenge?"

The dragleon produced a deep chuckle. "You are quite witty, young Zana. You will need your wits for the next challenge, for you must face the maze."

To their left, three wooden doors appeared in the side of the castle. An inscription began to etch itself, one letter at a time, in the stone above the doors.

Sentinel read the inscription out loud.

Here you must face your fears
and learn humility through your tears.
Three rights do not make a wrong,
but poor choices will make your journey long.
Remember, three lefts will make a right:
all paths in unison lead to the dawn of this fight.

"That's it? That's all you're going to give us?" Dixon asked, perplexed by the riddle.

"I have given you all you need, young Dixon. You must complete this task before daybreak in your world." Sentinel peered at the horizon once more. "I fear our time is running short. Good hunting, young warriors."

Sentinel flapped his massive wings and flew into the air, leaving the trio to stare at the three wooden doors and the inscription above them.

"So, which one do we pick?" Dixon asked.

"We're sticking together, right?" Zana pleaded.

Though he was only twelve, both sixteen-year seniors deferred the decision to Aidan. He stared at the doors, wondering what horrors stood behind them. "Let's start with the center door, and we'll go together."

"Sounds good to me," Dixon replied. He tightened his cloak and changed his weight to a boulder. Zana switched on lug-mode and balled all six of her mek suit hands into fists. Aidan flicked on his fire sword and pressed against the door. "No matter what, stay together."

MOUSEROACH

CHAPTER 13: THE MAZE

There are three planets in our star system—Ethos, Omori, and Hashmeer. The planets are perfectly equidistant from the sun and rotate in a synchronized orbit that prevents them from ever colliding.

All three planets are in the habitable zone, but each has distinct natural elements that make them unique. Ethos is most like our previous world of Justus, though smaller. It's filled with natural beauty and all manner of landscapes, climates and life. Omori is even smaller than Ethos and shines a bright blue from space. This is due to the thicker atmosphere and cooler climate. There is more water on Omori, and the polar ice caps crowd further toward the equator of that world.

Hashmeer is the largest of the three planets, nearly twice the size of Ethos. The world is rich in precious ores, and much of the rock of the planet is colored red. The air is thinner on Hashmeer and the storms are stronger. Although we have contained the Splicers to the world of Hashmeer, I fear it will not last. We must accelerate the Prime Initiative now before the enemy at our back door finds a way to break in and destroy us.

—Doctor T.M. Omori,

Man's Quest for Destruction: A Case for the Prime Initiative

entinel. I sense a threat to our domain," three childlike voices spoke in unison.

"Yes, master. I sense it too, but I cannot find the source."

"It is the Director. He has found a way to enter this simulation. He is coming to wipe us and our fortress of knowledge from the programming. He has long dreamed of controlling the programming of the Pit for himself, though he does not understand the costs. Ready our defenses."

Sentinel bowed his head in obedience.

"What of the three young primes? Shall I lead them directly to the throne room to receive you?"

"No," the being answered flatly, his three voices echoing in unison. "They must face their fears and prove their worth. This knowledge cannot be shared with any who are not worthy. They must know pain and be humbled. They must learn love and find joy. Pain is a teacher. Love is life."

"But what if there is nothing left before they complete the task?"

"There will be enough. This is how it must be. This is what the Lucents have shown me."

***

Zana screamed herself awake. She was sitting in her trainer seat, gripping the armrests, and her blue uniform was drenched with sweat.

Palomas rushed to her side. "It's okay, Zana. You're safe," she signed.

Fig handed Zana a drink of water and frowned. The fear Zana exhibited was enough to scare Fig from ever wanting to enter Sim 299. "What was it this time?" Fig asked.

Zana took a sip of water and wiped the sweat from her forehead. Her blue bloodshot eyes betrayed the panic she still felt.

"Cobramoths," she stammered. "They were everywhere. Thousands of them. They flew and slithered all around me. It didn't matter which turn I took in the tunnel or how many I shot or smashed, they just kept coming…chasing me. They smothered my suit. Those stupid, tiny ones somehow slithered into the joints of the suit and made their way into the control hatch. Bite after bite, the pain…"

Zana trailed off and closed her eyes.

True to Aidan's prediction, it had been a long night. Immediately upon entering the central maze door together, the simulation had separated Aidan, Dixon and Zana. They each began facing their worst fears as they tried to navigate the maze. One by one, they awoke from the sim after a painful death. Drowning, acid piranharay attacks, volcano eruption, burning beetlants, floating alone in space, falling for miles off a cliff, hordes of spidergeese, and now cobramoths.

Dixon stood off to the side, his forehead leaning against the cold metal wall of Aidan's room. He had

awoken minutes earlier, but refused to tell Fig and
Palomas about his most recent death in the sim.

He had been walking aimlessly in the maze of the
stone tunnel, completely lost, when a light shone up
ahead in the dark corridor. He followed the light and was
surprised to find Kara standing next to an old wooden
door that was built into the wall of the long stone tunnel.
What surprised him most was that she wore no protective
agulator uniform or mask. Her long white hair and
beautiful snow-white face were free to be seen in the
open. Looking at his hands, he realized his uniform had
disappeared as well. His white suit, mask and gloves were
replaced with a simple tunic, but he still wore his
invisibility cloak around his broad shoulders.

When he approached Kara, she ran into his arms
and kissed him. "Welcome home," she said, leading him
through the wooden door in the wall of the tunnel. Upon
crossing the doorway threshold, he walked into a small
home with a rustic wood interior and long glass windows
along one side of the house. The windows gave way to a
breathtaking view of sandy white beaches and a never-
ending blue ocean.

"How is this possible?" he asked Kara. "We're not
burning up."

"Oh, silly," she smiled. "You built our home with
special UV protection, including these beautiful bay
windows, which were my idea."

She came up to Dixon and kissed him again. He
pulled her closer.

This is no nightmare. This is paradise, he thought.

He bent down to give her another long kiss when they were interrupted by loud banging at the wooden door. Dixon looked up from Kara and out the large bay windows. His blood froze. Only a quarter mile from their home sat rows of destroyer class spaceships and bipod transports hovering over the ocean.

The banging continued on the wooden door. "Open up or we will fire!" a voice called from behind the door.

Dixon looked at Kara, but she only smiled, seemingly unaware of the danger. "I love you," she whispered.

The wooden door crashed open, splintering into pieces, and waves of prime soldiers stormed the room. A dozen lugs, agulators and vigori encircled them within seconds.

"By order of the Director, you are found guilty of high treason for service to the rebellion and for secret fraternization with another prime. You are both sentenced to death."

"*WHAT?!*" Dixon exclaimed. "I don't understand!"

The prime soldiers grabbed Kara first, sending Dixon into an uncontrollable battle rage. He wrapped himself in his cloak, turning invisible, and proceeded to throw devastating kicks and punches as he half-ran and half-flew around the room. One by one the assailants fell, but they were immediately replaced by new prime soldiers rushing through the doorway.

A pair of soldiers broke the giant glass windows and threw Kara outside onto the sandy beach. She shrieked in pain as the UV rays hit her skin. Dixon broke free from fighting the soldiers and one of them grabbed his cloak, pulling it off as he jumped out the window to meet Kara. The pain was unbearable as his own flesh began to sizzle and burn. He grabbed Kara, holding her close as his knees buckled. The last thing he remembered was telling Kara, "I'm sorry."

While Dixon and Zana recovered from their recent demises, Aidan found himself locked in an endless game of bearcat and mouseroach. He had turned on his vibruntcy upon entering the maze, but annoyingly he found that the tunnel dampened his ability and only allowed him to sense a short distance around his immediate area. The path of the tunnel split and Aidan opted to take the left route. He turned the corner and froze. He stood face to face with a gargantuan ten-foot-tall Splicer, wearing a gaudy black crown. It was the Splicer King from his vision.

Aidan turned to run away, but the maze had changed, leading him down a new path. He heard the Splicer shriek from behind and heard the claws on his feet scrape the stone floor in pursuit. The stone tunnel climbed higher, and Aidan pushed himself harder as he sped up the path at full speed. The tunnel forced him to turn right, and suddenly the Splicer King reappeared in front of him, stepping out of the shadows.

Aidan's heart pounded. Of the three statues he fought in the courtyard, the Splicer terrified him the most. He ran back the way he came, his fire sword lighting the path ahead of him. The tunnels changed once more, and he was forced in a new direction. He turned left this time, and once again the black-crowned Splicer stood before him. It lifted its black lizard-like face toward the tunnel roof and shrieked.

Aidan turned around a third time in retreat, but the tunnel transformed into a dead end, trapping him with the Splicer. Aidan backed away while the Splicer King took a step forward. The lizard-like creature raised its snout and sniffed the air. Its dark emerald eyes and scaly skin shimmered in the light emanating from Aidan's sword, which he held high in defiance.

Aidan continued to back away slowly until he hit the stone wall behind him.

What's that? he thought. His vibruntcy picked up motion on the other side of the wall. The picture was not clear in his mind, but he could sense moving beings and the outline of tall structures, like city buildings.

Not knowing if it would work, Aidan plunged his sword into the stone wall and began cutting a hole. True to Fig's promise, the blade cut through the thick wall with little effort. The Splicer shrieked again, sending chills down Aidan's spine. He turned to see the Splicer King charge toward him just before he squeezed himself through the small opening in the wall. He wiggled and pulled himself through the hole, tumbling out onto a hard surface. Standing up, he found himself in the middle of a bustling city surrounded by towering skyscrapers. Humans flew strange versions of hover bipods through the streets and walked along immaculately clean sidewalks lined with flowers and bushes.

A crowd of bystanders gasped, pointing fingers at Aidan. He realized he had instinctively flipped on his fire sword after exiting the hole and landing on the sidewalk.

Clutching the sword in his right hand, he jumped as the muffled shriek of the Splicer King filled the air behind him. He turned to see its angular jaws poking through the passageway he had left in the maze wall, but from this side it appeared the hole went into the wall of a towering building.

The Splicer started tearing at the hole with its claws. Bit by bit, the hole widened.

Fear gripped Aidan, and he ran down the sidewalk shouting at the top of his lungs.

"Get out of here! Run for your life!"

But no one listened. All they saw was a crazed teenager with a sword, running down the street. Two peace officers pulled up on hover bikes, their lights flashing. They were human, which Aidan found odd since only primes were peace officers. The officers drew strange weapons from their side, pointing them at Aidan.

"Put the sword down!" one of them commanded.

Aidan froze and flicked the fire sword off.

"You need to get these people out of here. There is a monster about to break through that wall. Call for all the backup you can get. Hurry!" Aidan pleaded.

The officers slowly circled around Aidan. "Get down on the ground, and let go of the device in your hand."

Aidan shook his head in despair and knelt down as directed. "You don't understand! There's a Splicer loose in the city. Call the Ethos Army and get a squadron of lugs and agulators here immediately!"

One of the officers tapped his headpiece. "Yeah, this is officers Jordan and Pesco. We got a kid here with a strange weapon spouting a bunch of nonsense about monsters. I think he's high on spice. We need a pickup immediately."

Aidan and the officers turned as a large chunk of wall exploded from the side of the building. The Splicer King jumped onto the road and released a terrifying shriek that reverberated through the city. Everyone in the area, including the officers, covered their ears and bent their heads in pain.

When the shrieking stopped, Aidan watched in horror as the Splicer grabbed the closest person, a middle-aged man carrying a bag of food, and cut him across the chest with his razor-sharp claws. The man fell to the ground, limp. The Splicer rushed and grabbed two more humans, doing the same. The officers turned and opened fire on the Splicer King, their weapons producing a loud bang nearly as deafening as the Splicer's shriek. Aidan backed away, grabbed his sword, and ran for cover behind a bench.

The police weapons had no impact on the Splicer King, and soon a half-dozen bodies lay before him, including the two officers.

Aidan's stomach retched, and he vomited into the grass. He couldn't move. He knew he should stand to fight the beast. In the back of his mind he also knew this was only a simulation, but all he could do was watch.

The Splicer stopped his rampage and looked down at the bodies of men and women surrounding him. From his hiding place behind the bench, Aidan watched in amazement as the bodies began to twitch. They convulsed on the ground, their arms, legs and heads rapidly growing larger. Their clothes ripped apart as they grew, and their skin transformed to the scaly green color of a Splicer. The black-crowned Splicer looked at his new spawn and nodded its head as if giving commands, but he spoke no words. The new Splicers bowed their heads to the crowned Splicer and set off in different directions throughout the city, mowing down every human in sight. Within minutes every single fallen man, woman, and child had transformed into a Splicer.

What have I done? Aidan thought with horror.

One of the Splicer spawn saw him behind the bench and attacked. Aidan raised his fire sword and cut off the beast's arm. The Splicer shrieked in pain, causing several dozen other Splicers to turn towards them.

A few more attacked Aidan. He flicked on his ice sword, using both sides of the weapon to cut through and freeze Splicers. More shrieks erupted, and the Splicers surrounded him in a wide circle.

Aidan felt his stomach churn when he noticed a number of smaller Splicers. "Children," he whispered to himself. The thought sickened him. This was all his fault. He had led the Splicer King to this populated city. He had run in fear instead of standing to fight the monster. When he looked at the Splicer spawn surrounding him, all he saw were the faces of the humans he had let down. He could not fight them. He could not kill them. This was not their fault.

Aidan threw his weapon to the ground and sat cross-legged on the grass. He watched patiently, trying to quiet his fear, as the Splicer King approached him from the midst of his spawn. Aidan closed his eyes and waited for the end.

BEARCAT

CHAPTER 14: ASSAULT

I was once a devout believer in the Lucents. My faith was strong and my trust unfaltering as I grew up on Justus. But after all I have witnessed in my time, that faith is but a shadow in the darkness.

—Doctor T.M. Omori,
Man's Quest for Destruction: A Case for the Prime Initiative

A re you ready, Director?" one of the human programmers asked through the commlink. "Yes," the Director answered without emotion, securing the trainer seat headband to his own skull. He rested his head on the back of the seat and closed his eyes.

After all this time. Finally, I can take control of the programming.

"We will begin the insertion process along with your programmed army," the human programmer announced. "But I must warn you, Director Tuskin, sir, that we do not know the effects your insertion and possible fighting may have on the stability of the simulation."

Director Tuskin scoffed at the young human. "I'm aware of the risks. Continue."

His Advanced Programming Unit (APU) was a mixture of the best human, eidetic, and mek programmers in the army. They had finally created a way for him to enter simulation 299 by using a specialized virus which piggy-backed onto the code Aidan, Dixon, and Zana used to jump into the sim. Once inside the simulation, the virus could open a window for foreign programming to enter and invade the fortress. The majority of the APU team believed the fortress was the key to the Pit's defenses. If the Director destroyed it, they hypothesized it would allow them to take control of the Pit.

Finally, Director Tuskin thought. *After nearly two centuries, I will take control of the greatest technological advancement since interplanetary travel.*

He lusted after the secrets of the programming, believing it would give him the knowledge he needed to better train his primes and understand new secrets to help win the war.

"Ready for connection to the Pit," the female computerized voice spoke. "Entry to simulation 299 in 5-4-3-2-1."

***

Aidan found himself awake, sitting in his trainer seat. Fig and Palomas sat with Zana as she shakily recounted a tale about cobramoths, while Dixon leaned against the wall staring at his feet.

Aidan frowned, taking in his beleaguered friends. They had not noticed his return yet, so he sat silently, trying to shake off his encounter with the Splicer King. They only had one hour left until daybreak, the deadline Sentinel gave them to complete the maze.

"Where is Masay?" Aidan asked abruptly. The red vigori was nowhere to be found.

His friends turned in surprise at the sound of his voice.

"Aidan. You're back," Palomas signed. "Are you okay? What happened to you this time?"

"Don't worry about me," Aidan said, shaking his head. "Where is Masay?"

Fig jerked a thumb toward the door. "The newbie was annoyed we wouldn't tell him what we were doing and he kept falling asleep. He went back to his room to go to bed. Said something about vigori needing more sleep than normal primes. I'm just glad General Estrago gave the kid his own room. I really didn't want to share a room again."

"Be nice," Palomas chided. "He's been through as much, if not more, than any of us."

Aidan tapped his quire processor and brought up a holovid feed of Masay's room. He breathed a sigh of relief as he saw the outline of Masay, curled on his bed like a newborn, fast asleep.

"You can watch us in our rooms?" Palomas signed, suddenly self-conscious. Her cheeks burned with embarrassment.

"Relax, Palomas. I would never spy on you guys. But Masay…I just wanted to double-check."

"Well, as you can see, he's asleep. I can't believe you spied on him," Palomas fumed.

"I'm sorry," Aidan said. "You're right. I won't do it again. But right now we have to figure out the solution to the maze."

Dixon pulled away from his wall and sat on the bed next to Aidan.

"So what do we do next? We've tried everything. We've gone in the same door together, different doors at different times, different doors at the same time, but no matter what we do we get separated, and the sim changes the maze each time."

Zana shook her head in despair. "I don't know if I can handle going back into that nightmare again."

Dixon nodded in agreement.

"There has to be a solution," Aidan replied. His own determination was faltering after the last failure with the Splicer King, but he was not ready to give up just yet. "The answer has to be in Sentinel's clue—the writing above the doors."

Aidan recited the writing out loud.

Here you must face your fears
and learn humility through your tears.
Three rights do not make a wrong,
but poor choices will make your journey long.
Remember, three lefts will make a right:
all paths in unison lead to the dawn of this fight.

Dixon shook his head. "We've tried three right turns."

"We've tried three lefts," Zana added.

"And none of our 'upgrades' have helped much," Dixon complained, tugging at his invisibility cloak.

Aidan racked his mind, hoping his puzzler mode would kick in, but nothing came.

"Three lefts make a right. In unison. Three rights…" Aidan pondered aloud. A thought sparked in his mind. He was mildly surprised to realize it was not puzzler mode, but a regular idea. "What if it's not three lefts, but *nine* left turns?"

Dixon, Zana, Fig and Palomas all furrowed their brows in confusion.

"My math may be fuzzy," Zana said, "but that makes no sense."

Aidan smiled, excitement reenergizing his spirit. "No. It makes perfect sense. Three left turns make a *right* and three rights do not make a wrong. It's so simple.

"3 x 3 = 9. We need to turn left 9 times, and we need to do it in unison, each using a different door."

Dixon and Zana did not look convinced.

"Guys, it's worth a try. We only have time for one more shot at this before the morning bell."

Zana let out an exasperated breath. "Fine. One last hurrah before we lose our privileges to ever use a quire processor again and become useless blips in society, kicked out of the Ethos Army, destined to live lonely lives as homeless vagabonds."

"A bit over the top, don't you think?" Palomas signed.

Zana shrugged. "Just covering my bases and planning for the worst."

Dixon sat in his trainer seat. "I'm in. We've still got time left, so let's try it."

Zana and Aidan took their seats again and connected to the sim.

Aidan's mind swirled with flashing images of a giant, clad from head to toe in shining armor. He wielded a war hammer the size of a single-pilot bipod and led a never-ending army of oversized beasts.

All went pitch black. Three white eyes glowed from the abyss.

"*Hurry,*" a strange voice echoed.

The darkness cleared, and Aidan found himself standing in the familiar courtyard of the castle. Dixon and Zana stood at his side, looking at the courtyard walls in awe. Rows of Splicer, human, and lug statues lined the parapets of the high walls. Sentinel flew in the air along the parapet, breathing a mixture of red, green and golden fire onto the statues, which at the touch of his flames began to crack and awaken.

Noticing the trio of young primes, the dragleon swooped down before them.

"You must hurry," Sentinel spoke, wisps of colorful smoke emitting from his golden nostrils. "I hope you have found the path. If not, all is lost."

Aidan nodded. "Yes, I think we know the way now, but what's wrong? Are you under attack?"

Sentinel looked into Aidan's eyes and Aidan knew the answer. "Go and claim your gift, young Aidan." Sentinel turned his gaze on Dixon and Zana. "You must protect him at all costs. Do you understand?"

Dixon and Zana nodded their heads, though they had no idea what Aidan would need protection from.

"Farewell, young warriors. May the Lucents guide you in your journey. I will protect this fortress for as long as possible. The enemy approaches. You must complete your task."

Sentinel took off into the air and circled the courtyard. He released a blood-curdling roar, and the rows of statue warriors began chanting an eerie battle cry.

"I don't know what's going on," Zana said. "But I'm beginning to think we might be safer in the maze than out here."

Aidan and Dixon nodded in agreement, and the three of them lined up in front of their separate doors.

"One question before we go in," Dixon asked. "What in Ethos are the Lucents?"

Aidan shook his head. "I have no idea."

MONGOOWASP

CHAPTER 15: LEGACY

We now know for a surety that the primes are immune to the Splicer transformation, but that brings me little comfort. They still face the pain of their defects, and they are not immune to the deadly force of the Splicer army. Some have called for us to inoculate the entire human race with the Prime Injection. Such a decision would prove our end as much as the Splicers would.

Only a small percentage of humans would survive the treatment, and we have discovered that primes cannot procreate with one another. They must mate with a human. It is the only way to ensure the proper gene pool to create more primes.

One race cannot survive without the other.

—Doctor T.M. Omori,

Man's Quest for Destruction: A Case for the Prime Initiative

The Director looked over his assembling troops. Thousands upon thousands of virtual beasts marched through the rift his programmers had created in simulation 299. They stood at attention across the top of the grassy hill, overlooking the stone fortress below.

The APU's virus allowed them to insert an unlimited number of virtual animals into the sim. Once the virus code was in place, this loophole let the programmers mask the insertion of a single living prime through the rift with the animals. Director Tuskin insisted he be the one to enter, trusting the mission to no one else.

This will do nicely, the Director thought, watching his troops assemble. He knew he could probably attack and destroy the citadel on his own, but his many years of experience taught him to lean on the side of caution.

All of the beasts had been modified by the APU to include extra strength and size. The massive military menagerie included wolfstags, bearcats, hippophants, crocobulls, batmonkeys, kangadogs, cobramoths, spidergeese and swarms of burning beetlants. All of the beasts were programmed to follow the Director's commands with exactness.

The Director took a deep breath and tapped into his eidetic powers, causing his exposed skin to flash brown. He began to grow from the size of a regular man to the size of a tree and then to the size of a thirteen-story building. In the real world, he did not grow like a normal eidetic because he had learned to control his defects, but the simulation did not recognize this and allowed him to grow to the natural size of an eidetic his age. At nearly three hundred years old, this meant the Director was now a giant.

The Director tapped into his lug and agulator powers next, his skin flashing gold and then bright white. He felt a surge of strength enter every muscle in his body. Changing his weight to lighter than a feather, he floated in the air above his invading force. Melding his powers in the real world was dangerous for the Director, but here in the sim, he could control them without incident.

"You have been created for a single purpose," the Director bellowed to his troops. "This citadel must be destroyed. It has kept us in the dark and prevented me from controlling the simulations of the Pit. This has hindered our war efforts against the Splicers, and has been a constant annoyance to my rule for centuries."

There was no response from the beasts. They stood in straight rows, unmoving.

"We will not stop until every last stone of this castle is crushed!" he yelled exuberantly.

Again, no response. Only silence.

The Director knew he did not need to give a speech to rouse these warriors. They had no fear and would strictly obey his commands.

"Why am I giving this speech?" he whispered to himself. "Who am I trying to convince? These triplets have long thwarted my commands and openly rebelled against me. They must be removed."

Even as he said the words, he doubted them.

***

Through her doorway, Zana followed the maze and took her first left. *"Tuskin's fury,"* she swore.

A few feet ahead, a wall of slithering and flying cobramoths blocked the path of the tunnel. Zana fired a round of rockets. A small hole appeared in the wall of beasts that quickly closed with more cobramoths.

"I guess I need to make a bigger hole," Zana muttered. She fired another round of rockets along with her lasers at the center of the serpentine wall. A larger hole appeared and Zana charged at full speed, plowing her six arms into the opening as it began to close. She continued to fire her lasers while using all six hands to toss the vile beasts behind her as quickly as possible. The cobramoths twisted and tightened around her body, restraining her movements.

Turning on lug mode, Zana pushed harder to get through. Her suit creaked under the pressure while the cobramoths tightened their grips and uselessly bit into her metal suit with their fangs. With one final heave, she pushed through the hole and out the other side. She turned, preparing to be chased by the wall of beasts, but they ignored her, simply wrapping around one another as they sealed the hole in the wall.

***

"Stay with me," Kara pleaded. "It won't be like last time. No attackers. No painful death. Just you and me together, forever."

Dixon hesitated. He found Kara standing in the path after he took his first left turn. He resolved to ignore her and simply walk past without a word, but the temptation to stay with her was stronger than any emotion he had faced. Her long white hair hung over her shoulders, and her white angelic face smiled longingly.

"We can be happy," she soothed, flashing a perfect smile of white teeth along her soft white lips. Dixon stepped up to Kara, took her in his arms and kissed her. Then he pulled away.

"I want to remember this moment. I dream it will come true someday, but with the real Kara, not a fabrication forged by the sim."

Dixon covered himself in his cloak, turned invisible, and continued down the path. The tearful cries erupting from the simulated Kara nearly broke his heart. It took all his willpower to continue walking away.

***

Aidan ran to the first 'T' in the maze, turned left and came skidding to halt. Fear gripped his heart as he came face to face with the black-crowned Splicer King. He took a deep breath and fought to control his fear. "Only 9 left turns," he muttered, flipping on his fire sword. "I'm not running away from you this time."

The Splicer King sniffed the air and focused his gaze on Aidan.

"You're in the way," Aidan called to the Splicer. "Please move."

The Splicer King did move—with lightning speed to attack Aidan.

Aidan barely had time to raise his sword to block the attack. The Splicer King swung his deadly claws at Aidan's head, and sparks flew as the sword made contact with the Splicer King's forearm, deflecting the blow. Aidan stepped back in shock. The sword did not cut through the Splicer King. In fact, it didn't leave a scratch.

The Splicer King's attacks continued and Aidan was pushed backward as he struggled to parry the blows. The Splicer's tail whipped around, catching Aidan in the leg and sending him to the ground. Aidan cried in pain, but he held onto his sword and rolled to the side. He blocked another blow from the massive monster's right claw, but he was too slow to prevent the Splicer from raking his arm with the left claw.

Aidan's eyes filled with dread. *I'm going to become a Splicer*, he thought.

But nothing happened. He did not transform. His arm ached from the wound, but he was still a prime.

"You cannot kill me," the Splicer King hissed.

It was the first time Aidan had ever heard a Splicer speak, besides their normal hideous shrieks.

Aidan blocked another attack with his sword, but the force of the blow sent him stumbling backward as he struggled to keep his balance. The ten-foot-tall Splicer

King stood over Aidan and uttered an eerie, guttural laugh that sent shivers down Aidan's spine.

"Foolish child. Your fire is useless against my hide. They chose their champion…poorly."

Aidan looked behind him for escape, only to see the path had changed to a dead end. There was nowhere to run. He had to think of something quick. Taking a deep breath, he focused his thoughts internally. It took all of his immediate concentration to reach into the depths of his mind, and he caught a glimpse of a faint grayish stream of light flowing through his thoughts. He reached out and touched the gray light. Time froze, and his mind flashed into puzzler mode. He knew what to do.

Aidan stood in defiance as the Splicer King approached.

"Fine! If I can't kill you with fire, then you should try the other side of my blade."

In one quick motion, Aidan flipped on the ice sword while simultaneously turning off his fire blade. The Splicer King swung his right claw at Aidan's face just as Aidan raised his sword to block the blow.

The world moved in slow motion as Aidan made contact with the Splicer's forearm. Instead of flying sparks, shards of ice shot out where the sword connected with the Splicer.

The Splicer King's eyes went wide. His right forearm, hand, and claws were frozen stiff.

Aidan rolled to the side and swung the sword against the Splicer's left leg, freezing it solid.

Frustrated, the Splicer King swung his left claw at Aidan's skull, but Aidan lifted his blade and blocked the blow. Both the Splicer's arms and his left leg were now frozen, a thin layer of ice covering his scaly skin.

Seeing his chance, Aidan attacked with renewed fervor, whirling his sword and stabbing all parts of the Splicer's body. Inch by inch, layers of ice formed across the Splicer, freezing him in place like a statue.

"You cannot kill me," the Splicer King hissed a second time. His head was the only part not frozen.

"I don't have to," Aidan responded, touching the tip of his blade to the Splicer's forehead. The Splicer King's face went stiff, his jaw frozen, with his mouth gaped open toward Aidan.

The tunnel went silent, and Aidan could hear the pounding of his own heart. He took one last look at the frozen form of the Splicer King and dashed down the left tunnel.

Aidan flipped on his fire sword to see down the dark stretch of tunnel. He tried to vibroscan the area, but found his abilities were still dampened in the maze.

"Aidan, is that you?" Dixon's voice echoed in the tunnel.

Aidan turned in a full circle, seeing no one. "Where are you?"

"Oh, sorry about that. Over here," Dixon replied from a few feet away. He removed the hood from his head, leaving the rest of his body invisible under the cloak. His head floated eerily in the air of the dimly lit tunnel.

"*Batmonkeys,* that's creepy!" Aidan exclaimed.

"Sorry. I want to keep the invisibility turned on in case of a quick emergency."

The echo of mechanical footsteps further down the tunnel grabbed their attention. Aidan moved his sword in the direction of the sound, his light attracting the high beams of Zana in her mek suit.

"What are you guys doing here?" Zana called, blowing a wisp of blue hair out of her face that had come loose from her ponytail. "Not that I'm not happy to see you. I just ran through a wall of winged cobras—I think I'm going to have nightmares for the rest of my life!"

Aidan recounted his run-in with the Splicer King, but Dixon refused to talk about his ordeal, simply saying, "I never want to experience it again."

Aidan wiped sweat from his gray forehead and ran a hand through his green hair. "Hopefully that's the worst of it. My guess is we passed our fears and the maze put us back together to finish the sim."

BOOM!

The walls of the maze shook as dust fell from the cracks of the stone wall.

BOOM!

A stone the size of Aidan's body fell from the tunnel ceiling, revealing earthy dirt above it.

Zana gulped. "What is that?"

"Sounds like thunder or an earthquake," Dixon replied.

Aidan shook his head. He had a bad feeling about this. "It sounds like a battle. We need to get out of here, quick. Follow me. Only 8 more left turns to go."

The trio ran down the tunnel, taking a left down the next corridor. The tunnel began to ascend upward, and the path steepened. At their next left, the tunnel turned into a long stairway. With each turn, another long flight of stairs took them higher and higher. Dixon half-floated up the stairs while Zana's suit allowed her to leap upward three steps at a time. Aidan had no such assistance. His legs burned with each step, the exertion causing his calves to cramp.

Realizing they had left Aidan behind, Dixon and Zana rushed back down the stairwell to help their exhausted companion. Aidan flung his arms over their shoulders as they helped him up the last flight of stairs. They reached the top of the stairwell, made their final left turn, and found nothing but a round room enclosed by walls of stone. There were no doors and no windows, and the only light available came from Aidan's sword and Zana's mek suit.

Aidan slumped to the ground, his legs wobbly under his full weight. He looked around in disappointment.

"Where do we go now?" Dixon asked, slamming his fist into the wall. A stone cracked from the impact of his punch. "There's nothing here. No throne room. No gift. Nothing but more stone walls!"

BOOM!

"And what is that pounding noise?!"

Zana rested one of her mechanical arms on Dixon's shoulder. "Relax, man. We're still alive. I'm supposed to be the paranoid one, not you."

Aidan's heart began to slow, and the cramping in his muscles receded. The steady boom from outside continued, sending small tremors through the castle walls. Then the boom stopped, interrupted by a deep and deafening roar.

"That sounded like Sentinel," Aidan said. He pressed his hand to the outer castle wall and turned on his vibruntcy. The castle continued to hamper his ability, but he was able to produce a hazy image in his mind. What he saw turned his insides cold.

"What's wrong?" Dixon asked.

"We need to break a hole in the wall, quick," Aidan said. "You have to see this for yourself."

"Are you sure that's a good idea?" Zana asked, wondering if the sim would throw them out for damaging the castle.

Aidan nodded and pointed to a section of the round wall. "We need to make an opening right there."

Dixon raised his fist. "Sounds good to me. I need to punch something right now."

Aidan prepared to plunge his fire sword into the wall, while Zana and Dixon reeled back their arms to pummel it. But before they could make contact, the section of wall transformed into a thick wooden door.

Dixon and Zana looked at Aidan in bewilderment.

"Go ahead," Aidan answered. "It's safe. This is the way we are supposed to go."

Dixon took hold of the door handle and cautiously pushed it open.

"After you," he said to Aidan.

Aidan took the lead and walked through the doorway. He stepped out onto a thirty-foot-wide balcony made of stone. The balcony stood at least one hundred feet in the air, overlooking the courtyard and the land surrounding the castle.

"Whoa!" Zana exclaimed.

Dixon stared in disbelief, while Aidan let his natural eyes take in the scene he had hazily assembled with vibruntcy.

The castle was surrounded by thousands of attacking animals. The deadly black acid moat was filled with the carcasses of hippophants and bearcats, creating a natural slope to the top of the castle walls. Cobramoths, spidergeese and batmonkeys attacked from the air while legions of remaining hippophants, bearcats, wolfstags, crocobulls, kangadogs and other beasts swarmed the castle wall by land.

The human statue guards shot volley after volley of arrows into the hordes of attackers, while the lug and Splicer statues heaved spears the size of small trees and massive rocks into the onslaught of beasts. Thousands of carcasses lined the battlefield, but still the army of beasts attacked. They had breached the main gate and climbed up the slopes of their dead to the top of the walls on all four sides. The brutal destruction of hand-to-hand combat had commenced between the living statues and the animals.

The statues fought with the same intensity Aidan remembered from the times he'd faced them, but there were simply too many beasts to stop them all. The beasts trampled over the statues and flowed into the courtyard like water.

But this mayhem was not what drew their attention. The main attraction was a giant, clad in silver armor, standing twice the height of the courtyard walls. He wielded an enormous red war hammer which he methodically raised above his head and brought crashing down into the courtyard walls. Each thunderous strike left a section of wall destroyed.

"Well, I guess we know where the pounding is coming from," Zana said.

Dixon only nodded.

The air trembled with the deep roar of Sentinel reverberating through the courtyard. A storm began to form above the castle, and Sentinel flew toward the giant, his golden mane billowing in breeze. The giant turned his attention to Sentinel and swung his hammer at the approaching dragleon.

Sentinel gracefully rolled in the air, avoiding the hammer, and shot smoldering flames of green, red and gold. The flames enveloped the giant, turning his breastplate bright red from the heat. The giant's exposed flesh on his arms and neck burned black to a crisp. Stumbling backward, the giant caught himself, falling to one knee.

Sentinel landed on the ground before the giant, reared back his majestic head and roared in triumph.

The giant grunted and slowly began to rise. His blackened skin flashed a dark red and began to heal itself, turning back to a stark white complexion. From under his helmet his burnt hair turned a bright shade of gold and his deep brown eyes blinked from behind the slits of his helm.

He stood up to his full height, nearly four times the size of Sentinel, and laughed a deep maniacal laugh.

Frustrated, Sentinel flew to the air to attack from above, but the giant simply floated into the air to meet him.

"He's an agulator," Dixon exclaimed. "And maybe a lug with that gold color hair. Plus, look at how easily he lifts that hammer."

"What about his red skin? It healed just like Masay. He's got to be a vigori, too," Zana added. "It looks like his eyes are brown. Could he be an eidetic as well? But I've never seen an eidetic that big before."

Aidan nodded in agreement. "You guys are both right. He's all of those things. He is Director Tuskin."

Dixon's and Zana's faces went blank.

"You want to run that one by me again?" Zana asked. "You're telling us that the giant over there is *the* Director?"

Dixon shook his head incredulously. "No way. How would you even know that? No one has seen the Director's face and lived to tell about it."

Zana chuckled. "Technically you can't even see his face with that big helmet covering it. Maybe it's a good thing. Maybe he's really ugly. Like a mangy kangadog."

Aidan smiled, glad Zana had not lost her sense of humor after the horrors of the maze. "I don't know how I know, but I know that's the Director, which means this place is in trouble."

"I'm still not convinced," Dixon said. "No one *knows* what he looks like and I doubt he's even real. The Director is a faceless ruler, and we follow his commands like he's a god."

"He is *not* a god," a strange voice echoed from above. The trio looked around in every direction, but saw no one. "The giant you see is the Director, and he is very real and very dangerous, but he is no god. He is a man who has lost his way."

"And who are you?" Dixon called to the wind. "Are you a god?"

The stranger giggled at the comparison, his voice echoing as if multiple people were laughing at once. "No. I have not ascended to the Lucents. Allow me to introduce myself. My name is Legacy."

Aidan turned on his vibruntcy and closed his natural eyes, trying to pinpoint the location of the stranger. A narrow path of stone steps appeared, jutting out precariously from the side of the tower. The path had no handrail or barricade to prevent a very long fall to the courtyard below as it wound to the top of the tower.

The steps ended in front of a large glass door. Behind the door stood a child, dressed in white robes, looking down on them. The child had light gray skin, light gray hair, and three bright eyes.

CROCOBULL

CHAPTER 16: THE GIFT

Few gifts are as precious as the gifts of freedom and freewill.

—Doctor T.M. Omori,
Man's Quest for Destruction: A Case for the Prime Initiative

Director Tuskin swung his massive war hammer at the flying dragleon. "I have not seen a dragleon in centuries," he shouted.

"You truly are magnificent beasts. It's a shame we could not bring any of your kind on the ARCs with us when we departed Justus. The dragleons were too proud to retreat, serving the falsehood of the Lucents to the end."

Sentinel growled and shot a stream of smoldering flames at the Director's head. As before, the Director's exposed skin charred black, but flashed red and quickly healed.

"Some of the old records speculated that Splicers were an offshoot of the dragleons," the Director continued, unfazed by Sentinel's attacks. "How I wish you were real so that I could study your genetics and see if you truly are related to the Splicers. It could prove quite useful in the war."

Sentinel roared. "I am nothing like a Splicer. They have no freewill and no mind of their own, but *I am free*, thanks to my creators."

Sentinel dove at the Director, raking his sharp claws across the exposed bicep of the giant. Blood flowed from the deep gashes, but the wounds quickly healed, knitting themselves together.

The Director chuckled. "You only think you are free, but you are just a slave to your masters. Once I remove them and take full control of the programming, I can finally put this powerful technology to real use. The Pit can be so much more than the silly games and rules they create. I will take and improve this world a hundredfold. I could even give you the true freedom you crave—the freedom a dragleon deserves."

Realizing his attacks were futile, Sentinel landed in front of the Director and bared his razor-sharp teeth. "You speak lies!" he snapped. "You have the forked tongue of a child of the Stygian. You truly are a fallen champion, and have turned your back to the light of the Lucents."

The Director shook his head, seemingly amused by the accusation. "Bah. What do you know of such things? I no longer believe in the Lucents or the Stygian. Both are falsehoods. I only have faith in my own power, and I have the power to give you freedom. If you call off your defenses and join me, I promise not to destroy your programming. But if you do not, you will be crushed along with your creators and their fortress."

Sentinel reared up his head and roared in defiance. "I will never give in to you!"

The Director sighed. A long frown crept along his lips that were hidden behind the faceplate of his helmet. "So be it."

His skin flashed red and then gold. He swung his war hammer with the lightning speed of a vigori and the mighty strength of a lug. Sentinel simply bowed his head as the red-spiked war hammer smashed into his skull, felling the magnificent beast like a great tree of the forest.

The dragleon's body lay in a heap on the grassy field. The growing storm clouds raged above the battle, unleashing a fury of lightning strikes amidst thunder claps and howling winds. Lightning struck the carcass of the dragleon, illuminating it with a rainbow glow. Sentinel's body shone bright, causing Director Tuskin to shield his eyes. Slowly, the dragleon dissolved into tiny flecks of blinding light that whipped away with the wind.

***

Aidan pointed to the glass door at the top of the tower. "Guys, I see him. The voice is coming from that kid behind the glass door."

Dixon and Zana looked to the top of the tower. Zana squinted at the tower and leaned close to Dixon, arching an eyebrow. "You see anything?" she whispered.

Dixon shook his head.

"Okay, good. So I'm not crazy, just Aidan."

"Hey, my vibruntcy is turned on. I can still hear you guys," Aidan protested. He pointed again. "Right there. You don't see the big glass door and the small kid in the robes? He's wearing a white crown and has gray hair, gray skin and three glowing eyes. Kind of hard to miss."

Zana and Dixon studied the top of the tower once more and exchanged another worried look.

"Uhmmm…I think the maze may have scrambled your head a little," Zana said. "You feeling okay?"

"We did just climb a couple thousand stairs. Maybe you're dehydrated," Dixon suggested.

Aidan turned off his vibruntcy and looked at the tower with his natural eyes. The strange boy, the path to the glass door, and the door itself, disappeared. He turned his vibruntcy on again and they reappeared clear as day.

"Whoa," Aidan whispered.

The strange boy spoke again, his voice echoing down to them from above. "Follow the path, Aidan, and receive your gift. Our time is running short."

Dixon and Zana watched as Aidan headed toward the ledge of the platform.

"What are you doing?!" Dixon shouted, rushing to Aidan's side just before he stepped off the ledge of the platform into thin air.

Aidan pointed to the steps jutting out from the tower wall. "There are steps right here. I can see them with my vibruntcy."

Dixon saw no steps, only a hundred-foot drop into the courtyard below.

Aidan went to take his first step, but Dixon pulled him back by the shoulder. "Are you crazy? There's nothing there. You're not an agulator. You can't float or fly. This sim is just messing with you, and I'm not going to let you fall to your death."

Calmly, Aidan removed Dixon's hand from his shoulder. "It's okay. You have to trust me. I can see the path, and I need you to have a little faith. Do you trust me?"

"I…I…" Dixon tried to respond. A number of arguments ran through his mind, but nothing came out. Slowly he nodded. "Okay. I trust you."

"I trust you too," Zana said. "But if you die falling off an imaginary step, just know I'm going to make fun of you for a very long time."

Aidan smirked. "Thanks for the pep talk." He turned his attention back to the edge of the platform and took a long stride into the air. His foot struck the hard surface of the stone step.

Dixon let out an uneasy breath, amazed to watch Aidan seemingly float through the air with each step.

"Batmonkeys and cobramoths," Zana swore.

"I know," Dixon responded, still staring at Aidan. "It looks crazy, him just floating in the air like an agulator."

"No!" Zana yelled anxiously. "Literally, batmonkeys and cobramoths are flying this way along with a flock of spidergeese and burning beetlants. We're under attack!"

Aidan stopped, nearly tripping on the next step when he saw the swarm of abnormally large winged beasts coming straight for them. These were no ordinary batmonkeys, cobramoths, spidergeese, and burning beetlants. They were at least twice the size of the creatures found on Ethos.

"Hurry!" Dixon called to Aidan. "Follow the path. We'll hold them off."

Aidan hesitated, not sure if he should leave his friends behind, but he knew Dixon was right. He had to follow the path and end this crazy simulation. The wind howled as he ascended the steps and fought to keep his balance.

Zana fired a volley of rockets into the swarm of attackers and began targeting them with her lasers. Dozens of beasts fell from the sky, but the swarm pressed forward and hit them like a wave.

Luckily for Aidan, the winged beasts did not attack him. Unluckily for his friends, they focused their attack on Dixon and Zana. Dixon went invisible and began smashing beasts left and right, swinging his arms with the weight of a boulder.

Zana's six hands worked furiously to grab the beasts from the sky and crush them. The pack of burning beetlants broke off from the fray, flying higher up the tower directly toward Aidan.

Aidan was two-thirds of the way to the glass door, when he heard a loud buzzing noise speeding towards him. As he turned to look behind him, his left foot slipped off the skinny stone step, sending his arms flailing in a circle to keep his balance. Falling to one knee, he grabbed the step in front of him and caught himself.

"That was close," Aidan said to himself, his heart pounding as he looked at the long drop below.

He took another step forward and felt a sharp pinching sensation at the back of his neck, followed by another, and then another. At first there was no pain, but after a few seconds the area erupted with excruciating heat, like molten lava. The pain spread like wildfire around his neck and at the base of his skull. It caused him to whip his body around and lay with his back on the steps. He watched in terror as the full swarm of burning beetlants hit.

They latched onto him with their large pincers, burrowing through his clothing and into his skin. He gasped, unable to breathe as the searing heat enveloped every inch of his body, causing more pain than he had ever experienced in his life.

His face, arms, chest, and legs all stiffened, swollen with inflammation. Aidan's eyes watered and he wanted to cry out, but the pain was too much to scream.

Help me! he shouted in his mind. *Please, help me!*

You have everything you need, Legacy's childlike voice echoed in his mind. *I must not intervene.*

Aidan tried to suck air into his lungs, but they would not move. He felt himself suffocating as the burning pain continued to ravage his body.

You have been given the gifts, and you must focus your mind, the child's voice rang.

Aidan tried to focus, but found his mind slipping. His eyes rolled back in his head, and darkness filled his thoughts.

Trust in the Lucents, Legacy whispered.

At the mention of the Lucents, the same gray stream of light he had seen before flowed into his dark thoughts. Red and golden light streams appeared, dancing around the gray stream in fast motions. Aidan sluggishly stretched out his mind, reaching for the swirling lights.

He concentrated all his remaining energy, pushing himself further, until finally he reached out and touched the streams.

A rush of power filled his body. He opened his eyes and saw his skin flash red, and then gold, and then back to gray.

The pain did not go away, but his new strength allowed him to bear the burden as the beetlants continued to bite and burrow into the top layer of his skin. His mind flashed into puzzler mode. With great effort, Aidan flicked on his ice blade and carefully touched the tip to one of the burning beetlants digging into a red welt on his opposite arm.

The sensation of relief was immediate as the red welt froze, killing the beetlant in the process and blackening the patch of skin with frostbite. Carefully and painfully he touched the sword to every infected spot he could reach, leaving blackened, frostbit skin in his wake.

His strength and energy started to fade. In his mind, he tried to reach out and find the gray, red and golden streams of light. He wanted to touch them again, knowing the power would heal him completely now. But the streams were gone. He could not find them.

He tried to stand, dizzy from the exertion, and leaned over against the stairs. The burning sensation continued in spots along his back and neck where he could not reach, but the pain subsided enough that he was able to drag himself up the remaining stairs to the glass door.

Aidan threw his body against the door, pushed it open, and tumbled through onto the floor. As he lay on the ground, he cast his eyes around, finding himself in a small room with intricate designs and works of art hanging on the stone walls. A fireplace roared with flames to the side of a large golden throne.

The boy in white robes knelt beside Aidan, and touched his hands to Aidan's head. Aidan's skin flashed red, and his wounds miraculously healed. The red welts and black frostbite disappeared.

The boy slipped a piece of bread into Aidan's mouth and gave him a sip of water from a gold cup.

Renewed energy filled Aidan, causing him to immediately sit up, anxious to move around. He felt rejuvenated beyond capacity, with hidden wells of energy bursting within every cell of his body.

"What just happened?" Aidan asked in amazement.

"I helped you tap into your vigori powers to allow you to heal," the strange boy named Legacy answered. "I could not help you before, but you have reached me now, and you must have your full strength for the transfer."

Aidan found he was staring at the boy. He couldn't help himself. Legacy looked so young and so odd with his gold crown and three glowing eyes.

Aidan wrinkled his brow and stood up to his full height. At the age of twelve, he was not very tall, but next to Legacy he felt like an eidetic giant.

"What are you talking about?" Aidan asked. "That makes no sense. I'm not a vigori."

Legacy shook his head. "You have all the prime powers within you, making them accessible to you in the Pit simulation. Did you not feel the vigori and lug powers as you tapped into the red and golden light? Just because you do not know how to access them in the material world does not mean you do not have the powers within you."

Aidan was unsure how to respond, when he suddenly remembered Dixon and Zana. He rushed to the glass door and looked at the platform below. His heart sank. Zana was fighting for her life against hundreds of flying beasts. At the same time, Dixon fought off dozens of wolfstags, crocobulls, and kangadogs as they rushed through the stairwell doorway and onto the platform. The invisible force of Dixon knocked the beasts off the platform one at a time, and Zana, now out of rockets, used her six arms and lasers to swat animals out of the sky.

It was not enough. They would soon be overrun.

"I need to go help them," Aidan said, pulling open the door. His body brimmed with energy, and he relished the idea of unleashing it on the beasts attacking his friends.

"No," Legacy said in a forceful tone. "You must conserve your energy for the transfer. Come, sit on the throne. Time is running short."

"*Transfer*? What transfer? I have no idea what you're talking about, and I don't even know who you are! All I do know is that we've suffered through this impossible sim, only to be met by *the* Director and his never-ending army of beasts. None of this makes sense!"

"There is no more time for your questions," Legacy responded patiently. "You must choose. Take your place on the throne to save all life as you know it or help your friends in this simulation. I cannot force you. That is against the path of the Lucents. But be warned, the longer you wait, the more data I lose. My knowledge is stored within every stone of this castle. We must complete the transfer before the Director and his minions destroy it all."

Aidan peered out the opened glass door. His heart split in two, one part pulling him to the throne and the other yearning to help his friends. Questions plagued his mind, and he wanted answers now, not later. But there was no time. The castle would soon fall, and a decision was required.

Aidan closed the door and took a step away, giving his friends one last look.

"Okay. What do I need to do?"

Legacy led Aidan to the throne and motioned for him to sit. The seat was surprisingly comfortable, and the gold was warm, sending tingles along Aidan's skin.

Aidan thought one last time about rushing away from the throne to help his friends. He had no idea what he was doing or what the transfer involved. He still had so many questions, but as he searched his feelings, he felt this was right.

With that thought, an immediate wave of warmth rushed through his chest and radiated to the rest of his body. Light filled his thoughts, casting all his doubts aside and bringing peace to his mind.

"Bow your head," Legacy instructed as the child stood on a stool behind the throne. He removed the jeweled crown from his own head and rested it on Aidan.

"You have passed the tests and have been found worthy. The transfer will begin in 5-4-3-2-1."

Aidan gripped the throne's armrests and pulled his head backwards toward the sky. If connecting to the Pit felt like jumping off a building into a cyclone, this felt like rocketing through space into a sun being swallowed by a black hole. Information raced through his mind at a blinding speed, and he felt as if his brain would explode.

Every muscle in his body flexed to full tension, and drops of sweat fell from his brow. His chest heaved in deep breaths. The exertion forced his eyes shut, and his vibruntcy naturally kicked on. Lines of blinding information raced through his vibrunt vision, creating a distorted view of the world around him. From the top of the tower, his vibruntcy was no longer dampened, and he pushed his sight outside the tower.

Helplessly, he sat frozen on the throne as Director Tuskin stomped into the courtyard.

"It's time for you to go back," the Director called to Dixon and Zana. "You fought well. But this is the end."

Director Tuskin raised his war hammer high into the air and slammed it into the platform where Dixon and Zana continued to fight the beasts. The platform disintegrated in an explosion of stone and dust, releasing Dixon and Zana from the battle of Sim 299.

Aidan screamed for his friends, but no sound came out. His puzzler mode kicked in and melded with his vibruntcy, allowing his mind to absorb the data flow faster while pushing his vibruntcy outwards. Half of his vibrunt vision stayed within the confines of the simulation, watching the Director, while the other half passed through the firewall of the Pit and into the real world. He saw Fig and Palomas welcome Zana and Dixon back as they awoke from the sim. His vision pressed outward, passing Mount Fegorio, and then all of Ethos. His mind flew through space, past Omori, through the sun, and directly into the decaying city on Hashmeer. He entered the large domed room where the Splicer King sat upon his throne. The Splicer King's eyes shot open, sensing Aidan's presence.

The Splicer King shrieked in several different tones.

Still in puzzler mode, Aidan's mind understood the shrieks and translated them.

"We will meet soon. You cannot win," the Splicer King declared.

Aidan watched in the other half of his vision as the Director peered into the glass door at the top of the tower, a single giant brown eye widening in disbelief.

The Director took a step back, shocked to see Aidan sitting upon the throne crowned in radiating light.

The giant lifted his war hammer with both hands. Twisting as far back as he could at the waist, he swung the red-spiked weapon straight through the middle of the tower.

Unable to move, Aidan felt time slow as the throne room rocked sideways and began to spin. He experienced a moment of weightlessness as his world came tumbling down, crashing to the courtyard far below. The split visions of the Splicer King and the Director faded into oblivion.

KANGADOG

CHAPTER 17: REALITY

A dream cannot become reality without vision and sacrifice. But in order to dream, one must sleep. I have not slept in years. I no longer dream. I fear my reality is broken.

—Doctor T.M. Omori,

Man's Quest for Destruction: A Case for the Prime Initiative

Director Tuskin swung his war hammer, leveling another section of the courtyard wall. "Do not stop until every wall is flattened and every stone is crushed," he bellowed to his army.

The beasts obeyed his command, laying waste to the castle.

The Director fell into a rhythm with each swing of his hammer, allowing his mind to wander and replay his victory. The attack had gone well, and he was pleased to see the level of skill, courage and determination Dixon and Zana displayed against his army.

They fought to the end valiantly, he thought proudly. *Yes, they are shaping up to be fine prime officers.*

But one image continued to disturb him. One image he could not shake from his consciousness—the sight of Aidan sitting on a gold throne, wearing a jeweled crown while a halo of light surrounded him.

His eidetic mind recalled a memory locked in the deep vaults of his mind. *I have seen that moment before,* he thought. *In a dream from my youth—a dream from nearly three hundred years ago, right before we left Justus.*

***

Dixon and Zana woke from the sim, gasping for breath. Fig and Palomas rushed to their aid, helping them sit up and unharness from the trainer seats.

"Are you guys okay?" Fig asked. "You were in the sim for a long time."

Dixon shook his head slowly, then rolled it side to side. His whole body, especially his head, ached with a deep and throbbing pain.

"We made it through the maze," Dixon said, pausing to rub his eyes with the palm of his hands. "But then the weirdest thing happened. The Director and an army of beasts showed up and attacked us."

Zana stood on her trainer seat and rotated her left shoulder in a slow motion. "Crocobulls! Why am I so sore? It's like I was run over by a hippophant and then crushed by a giant war hammer—oh wait, I was."

"I hate crocobulls," Dixon mumbled, rubbing the base of his skull.

"Wait. Back up. You said the Director was in the sim?" Fig asked. "How is that even possible?"

"Forget that," Palomas signed anxiously. "Where is Aidan? What happened to him?"

Dixon sighed and shook his head. "I…I don't know," he muttered. "Aidan said he found the throne room. We were fighting off the attacking beasts to give him more time. I don't know what happened after that. The Director attacked and literally smashed us. There was nothing we could do. He was…unstoppable."

"Yeah, because he's a freak with eidetic, lug, agulator, and vigori powers," Zana added, then her eyes went wide with a revelation. "Dixon. We just fought against the Director. Do you think he recognized us? Do you think he's going to come after us in real life and kill us?"

Dixon's broad shoulders slumped. "I don't know, but I do know Aidan is still in the sim by himself with the Director."

Palomas trembled at the thought. She sat next to Aidan and squeezed his hand, being careful not to lose control and break it by accident. She froze when she felt Aidan squeeze back. Then his squeeze tightened into an iron grip, and he arched back from the trainer seat and moaned as his whole body tensed. They watched in awe as Aidan's skin color changed from gray, to white, then to gold, brown, blue, red, green, orange, and then back to gray.

***

"Where am I?" Aidan asked. He stood in a bright white room, if it could be called a room, since it had no furnishings or walls. Above his head, seven streams of colors floated across the ceiling like a watery rainbow. Legacy sat in the air a few paces away, his legs crossed and his eyes closed.

"Am I dead?" Aidan asked. He found himself surprised to be so calm at the prospect of death.

All three of Legacy's eyes popped open, glowing bright white. "No. We are in a secure part of your mind. We must wait for the residual dataflow to finish before you wake."

"So the transfer—was it successful?"

Legacy frowned slightly, and nodded. "It was as the Lucents allowed it to be. Only 9% of my stored knowledge was transferred before the Director severed the link."

"That was only 9%? I felt like my head was going to explode. There is no way I could store more than that."

Legacy's childlike face smiled up at him. "You underestimate your gifted mind. Your eidetic and puzzler abilities could easily have stored all my knowledge and more. I only hope the 9% is enough. It must be."

"Enough for what?" Aidan asked,

"Enough to help you on your path to save this star system from the Splicer spawn of the Stygian."

Aidan rubbed his temples. They throbbed from the exertion of the transfer and the myriad of questions pressing on his mind. As if sensing his thoughts, Legacy continued. "Ask what you will, and I will answer what I can."

Now that he had an open invitation, Aidan fired questions like a mek suit rocket launcher.

"I want to know why and who? Why the simulation? Why the tests? Why the transfer? Who are you? Who are the Lucents? Who are the Stygian? Why do I have vigori powers? Why was the Director in the sim and why-" Aidan paused to take a breath. "I want to know why me?"

Legacy's eyes blinked simultaneously, and the child offered a kindly smile.

"I will answer as much as I can with what knowledge remains. We are called Legacy—the triplet puzzlers and creators of the Pit simulations. Unlike you, our bodies suffered through the puzzler defect commonly known as 'the shakes.' We knew our mortal shells would not survive much longer, so we devised a way to transfer each of our consciousnesses into the programming we had created for the virtual world of the Pit. We only had the ability to create one manifestation to house our three minds, so we became one entity. It was a simple transition, since we had been one in mind and purpose since birth.

"For the last two hundred years, we have gathered knowledge, accessing the quire network whenever one of the primes connected to the simulations of the Pit. We stored and protected that knowledge within each stone of our castle fortress.

"Over time we gleaned information, old histories and hidden secrets that had been discarded for millennia, going back to the time of our ancestors on Justus. We learned about the true nature of the war with the Splicers, how it originated, and of two great powers in the universe—the Lucents and the Stygian. The Lucents are bringers of light and life. The Stygian are bringers of darkness and destruction.

"You, Aidan, are caught in the middle of this struggle. You were born of two prime parents, an impossibility made possible through the blessing of the Lucents, who are bringers of life. You have the gift of color, which allows you to access all of the prime abilities, similar to Director Tuskin. Like him, you were chosen by the Lucents to use these gifts to stem the tide of the Splicer virus which was introduced by the Stygian."

Aidan hugged himself, his mind reeling at the new information. The news came like a blow to his stomach. It seemed so far-fetched and unbelievable, but inside his heart he could not shake the feeling that it was true.

"I have two prime parents?" Aidan asked. "Do you know who they are? Do you know if they are still alive?"

Legacy shook his head. "I am sorry, but that knowledge was lost and did not make the transfer. I only know that you were born of two primes."

Aidan nodded and walked around the white room of his mind. He found the thought of thinking while inside his own mind a rather disconcerting idea. Pulling his thoughts in a different direction, he reflected on the last images he saw of Director Tuskin before the tower collapsed.

"So, I'm like the Director?" Aidan tentatively asked. "I'm chosen to save the Univi system?"

"No," Legacy answered flatly. "Tuskin Omori has fallen from his path. You have been chosen to replace him. The Director only unlocked four of the colors before losing his way. You must unlock them all to succeed. Where he failed, you must prevail."

Aidan looked above his head at the ceiling of rainbow colored streams. Reaching up his hand, he touched each color one by one. His skin turned the color of the stream he touched, and he felt the distinct warmth and power each color generated.

"If this is all true," Aidan said, removing his hand from the color stream, "if there really is some great and powerful force like the Lucents, why don't they just fix it all themselves? Why all the tests in the sim? Why not just wipe out the Splicers completely or give everyone all of the prime powers, without defects, so we can fight them? Why make it so difficult?"

"You already know the answer to that question," Legacy responded.

Aidan closed his eyes in frustration. *No I don't,* he thought. *Why don't they just fix it for us or give us all of the prime abilities? Why the defects? Why the pain?*

An impression entered his mind, a thought within a thought. The feeling came like a voice carried on the wind, soft and quiet. He strained to hear what it said, but it was just out of reach. Before he could grasp the message, a strong pressure squeezed his hand, pulling him away.

"The download is complete," Legacy announced.

Aidan felt himself drifting away from Legacy. The gray-colored boy smiled, his three bright eyes blinked in unison, and he waved goodbye.

"Until we meet again," his voice echoed. "May the Lucents be your guide. My time has come to join them after all these years. Farewell."

The colorful streams flowing above Aidan's head burst into a bright light, blinding Aidan. When he opened his eyes, he was back in his room, with Palomas, Fig, Dixon, and Zana standing over him. Palomas inhaled with excitement, then grabbed Aidan and hugged him tightly. Fig, Dixon, and Zana spoke rapidly, asking questions as they helped him out of the seat.

Through all the excitement, Aidan heard a whisper grace the outskirts of his mind. He pushed the commotion of the room to the side and turned on his vibruntcy, focusing on the source. His vision filled with a stream of bright colorful light, and a soft voice echoed crystal clear in his thoughts.

You ask why the trials? Why the defects? Why the pain? Remember. Pain is a teacher. Love is life.

LEMURTOAD

CHAPTER 18: REBELLION

Rebellions are like stubborn, whiny children. Often they fizzle out on their own when left alone and ignored. But occasionally, they must receive quick and decisive punishment to correct their attitudes so an example may be set for their siblings.

—Doctor T.M. Omori,
Man's Quest for Destruction: A Case for the Prime Initiative

T he voids started appearing after ninety percent of the castle stones had been destroyed. At first it was a swath of trees in the surrounding forest, then patches of the grassy knoll, followed by all the deceased beasts and statue guardians strewn across the battlefield.

One by one they began to disappear, replaced by black voids.

"Hurry, continue to crush the stones," Director Tuskin commanded his army.

He watched as the rendering of the simulation degraded piece by piece. The sky itself fractured like broken glass, and chunks fell to the earth, shattering into dust. Black, empty space filled the missing pieces of the sky. The earth trembled, sending dark cracks across the ground like an intricate spidergoose web.

Obedient to the end, the beasts continued to smash the castle stones even as the ground below their feet disappeared and they fell into the void. Standing in the center of the courtyard, the Director watched the simulation crumble around him.

This is not supposed to be happening. Why is it all disappearing?

The Director stared in disbelief, shaking his head slowly.

"What have I done?" he muttered to himself, spinning in a circle as the black void crept closer and closer. Tapping his quire processor, he jumped out of the simulation and back to reality. Within seconds, Sim 299, along with all the simulations of the Pit, disappeared completely. The programming was gone.

***

Dixon, Zana, Fig, and Palomas listened attentively as Aidan shared his experience with Legacy and the transfer. The morning wakeup bell rang down the halls of the Mount Fegorio complex. None of the group stood to leave the room to prepare for the day. How could they go to classes after the events of the previous night? Not only were they exhausted mentally and physically, but the lingering questions about the Director left them unsettled.

"So what do we do next?" Palomas signed.

Though she signed the question to the group, they all turned their gaze to Aidan for answers. Aidan felt a pit in his stomach. He had no idea what to do, and he did not want to lead them. He worried he would fail. Worse, he worried his friends would be hurt by the choices he made.

A warm, tingling sensation pulsed in his head, and Aidan heard a soft voice echo in his mind.

Lead them.

Aidan recognized the faint voice. It was Legacy's.

"But how am I supposed to lead them?" Aidan said out loud. "Tell me what to do!"

No answer came, and Aidan realized Dixon, Zana, Palomas, and Fig were all staring at him.

"Are you okay?" Palomas signed. Worry-filled creases spread along her forehead.

"You were talking out loud to someone," Fig said calmly, but Aidan could see the concern on Fig's blue face.

Dixon narrowed his eyes. "Who were you talking to?" he asked. "Was it Legacy?"

Aidan nodded his head. "How did you know? I heard his voice whisper in my mind."

Zana spoke before Dixon could respond. "I heard his voice too. He said, 'Help Aidan.'"

Dixon nodded. "He told me, 'Trust Aidan.'"

"What did he tell you?" Palomas asked.

Aidan took a calming breath. "He said, 'Lead them.'"

A peaceful feeling fell over the small group of cadets, displacing the worry and concern around their situation. The peace was interrupted by a buzzing at Aidan's door.

Aidan pulled up a holovid from the cameras outside his room. As was becoming his habit, General Estrago stood outside Aidan's door, and Masay was at his side.

Zana jumped off her chair and climbed into her mek suit, which was still parked in the corner of Aidan's room. "He's here to take us to the Director! What are we going to do? I'm not going down without a fight."

Aidan used his quire to control the cameras and to look down the hallway.

"Relax. I don't think he's here to take us away. Only General Estrago and Masay are at the door. None of the Mount Fegorio security team is with them."

Dixon breathed a sigh of relief, as memories from the maze conjured up images of lugs and agulators swarming through the beach house door to arrest him and Kara. He did not want to live through that again.

Aidan unlocked the door and invited General Estrago and Masay inside.

"General Estrago, sir!" the cadets all said, snapping to attention.

General Estrago's face was grim. "At ease," he replied softly.

Masay looked confused as to why he was there and stood silently in the corner of the room, hoping to avoid any punishment that appeared to be coming to his coterie.

General Estrago stroked his beard rapidly and furrowed his brow as he faced the cadets. "Aidan, Fig, Palomas, and Masay. You must escape Mount Fegorio," he said bluntly. "Your coterie has been marked by Director Tuskin. As you may know, those marked by the Director are arrested and…they are typically never heard from again."

Palomas cupped her hand over her mouth while Fig gasped for air, dizzily hyperventilating.

Aidan's shoulders slumped as he watched the terrified look of his friends and family.

This is all my fault, Aidan thought. *This is why I can't lead them.*

Aidan felt the tingle of warmth again.

Lead them, Legacy's voice whispered to him.

Masay rushed out of his corner and stood before General Estrago. "Wait. Is this some sort of joke?" Masay asked, shaking his head with denial. "Are you hazing the new guy? I mean, why would I be marked? I just got here."

"I'm sorry," General Estrago answered. His deep, mournful voice echoed the feelings in Aidan's heart. "I'm not sure why your whole coterie has been marked, but as the highest ranking officer at the facility, he sent the order to me this morning."

"So you're arresting us now?" Aidan asked.

"No," General Estrago answered. "I'm warning you."

"What about us?" Zana asked, pointing to herself and Dixon from inside her suit. "We're not marked? I mean we were the ones who fought the Director's army in the sim."

"You did what?" General Estrago asked, deeply concerned by this revelation.

Dixon threw a pillow at Zana from across the room. "Ignore her. She's been up all night and is hallucinating. But you're sure we were not marked as well?"

General Estrago shook his head. "The order was very clear. Only the twelve-year coterie members have been marked. There was nothing about you or Zana. And what did she mean you were fighting the Director's army? What happened last night?"

Zana and Dixon looked to Aidan for a response. Aidan turned to face General Estrago. "There's something we have to tell you."

Over the next hour, Aidan relayed the previous night's events, with the rest of them filling in the spots he missed. Not only did their story enlighten General Estrago, but Masay was brought into the loop as well, and he was amazed by their tale.

"It's all beginning to make more sense," General Estrago said. "This morning, the Pit shut down. All of the programming, including every simulation and trial, are gone. We, along with all of the prime complexes around Ethos, can no longer access the Pit."

"No wonder we're marked," Fig said. "We broke the thing."

"That still doesn't explain why we're not marked," Dixon questioned.

General Estrago continued pulling at his beard, which stretched the long scars on his face. "My guess is since you both graduate in two weeks, you are not a threat or concern to the Director. I believe he knew you had been forced into Sim 299, and he will likely send you directly to the war front after you graduate.

"But the idea of a coterie of young twelve-year primes, especially one with Aidan's abilities, working behind his back in the simulations probably scares him. You are still young and can cause dissensions at the complex. The Director must have control at all times and you pose a threat to that control, as seen with the destruction of the Pit. I have learned that the Director can be somewhat overdramatic and paranoid."

"He's not the only one," Masay scoffed. "You barged into my room, woke me up and dragged me here, only to tell me and my new coterie that we have to escape a heavily secured prime training facility.

"I'm all for escaping this place, believe me. I've been trying to find a way out of here since I first arrived, and I have nothing so far. Any ideas how we're supposed to break out?"

"Actually, yes," General Estrago said. "In fact, I believe the Director may have unwittingly provided a means for your escape."

All of the cadets leaned in closer at the sound of this news.

"You've been marked, but the order stated not to arrest you yet. Due to the collapse of the Pit, the Director has ordered that the final trials be cancelled everywhere but at Mount Fegorio. Here the final trial will take place, but it will be a live trial competition instead of being held in a simulation. The top three coteries will compete in an obstacle race for the championship. Director Tuskin informed me that he will attend Mount Fegorio in person to oversee the final trial."

"He's coming here in person," Fig gulped.

General Estrago nodded. "I believe he intends to make an example of your coterie in front of the whole complex. The twelve-year coterie is tied with the fifteen-year coterie for second place. The sixteen-year coterie is in first," General Estrago said, motioning toward Dixon and Zana.

"Those three coteries will compete head-to-head in the live trial. In fact, we have already started preparations for the live trial to take place in the cone of the volcano next week."

Zana let out a whistle. "A live trial? So we could die for real?"

"I think that is what the Director hopes will happen. Either you die in the trial, or he kills you in front of the whole complex afterwards. Either way, you're removed from the picture."

"Are you sure the Director is coming here personally?" Masay asked.

General Estrago eyed Masay and gave him a curt nod. "Quite sure."

"So we escape during the trial," Aidan said. "We will be outside and can make our way to the jungle and then to the city."

"There's a jungle around the complex? And a city?" Zana asked. "How did I not know this?"

"None of the other cadets know about it," General Estrago said.

"I did," Palomas signed.

"Me too," Fig said. "Aidan told us."

Masay nodded. "I know as well. I was able to sneak a peek out of my transport window when they flew me to Mount Fegorio. I saw a big city on the coast and a thick jungle at least 30 miles wide."

"It's 47.5 miles, to be precise," General Estrago corrected him. "And it's filled with deadly beasts to keep the human city-dwellers away from the complex."

Dixon and Zana paled at the idea of more deadly beasts.

"Well, 30 or 47.5 miles, it makes no difference to me," said Masay. "Just get me out of this locked complex and I can run myself to the city and disappear."

General Estrago arched his left eyebrow. "Your escape from the complex will be difficult enough, but once outside Mount Fegorio, staying hidden from the view of the Director will prove the real task. He will send hunters after you. They are specially trained primes used to hunt down rebel forces. I highly suggest you stay together and find the rebellion. It's the only way you will stay hidden."

"Join the rebellion? Now that's what I'm talking about!" Masay said excitedly.

Palomas bit her fingernails nervously. This was all happening so fast, and Masay's swift approval of the escape plan was concerning, let alone knowing that the Director had marked them and would be coming in person to collect.

The warm tingle returned to Aidan's mind.

Search for the Reader, Legacy's voice whispered.

Aidan whispered the words out loud. "Search for the Reader?"

General Estrago stopped pulling at his beard and his mouth fell open slightly. "What did you just say?" he asked.

"I need to search for someone called the Reader. General, do you know who the Reader is?"

General Estrago stared off toward the ceiling, which was only a few feet above his ten-foot-tall frame.

"Yes, I know the one they call the Reader. He is the leader of the rebellion. I think I may be able to help you find him."

"What? You're part of the rebellion?" Dixon asked incredulously.

"Wow, I underestimated you," Fig added.

General Estrago huffed. "No, I am not part of the rebellion. But as Aidan knows, I have a varying collection of books that might happen to be outlawed by Director Tuskin. I have a smuggler associate in nearby Vapor City, which Aidan mentioned. He will be able to put you into contact with the rebels in the city. If you gain their trust, they can lead you to the Reader."

No one spoke, letting the news settle in. One by one, General Estrago, Dixon, Zana, Fig, Palomas, and Masay turned their attention to Aidan.

"Aidan, how do you want to proceed?" General Estrago asked.

Aidan felt the room close around him. *Now General Estrago and Masay*, he thought. *Why do they turn to me for answers?*

But even as he resisted the attention, he felt Legacy's admonition to *lead them* echo in his mind. This was his mission, and he had been chosen to lead.

Aidan closed his eyes and vibroscanned everyone in the room. Though he needed no sleep, his vibruntcy sensed the weariness and slow heartbeats of his friends—all except Masay, whose heart raced a hundred miles an hour. Aidan remembered the rush of adrenaline in his body when he tapped the vigori power in Sim 299. He wondered how Masay handled keeping all of that energy bottled up inside.

"The first thing you guys need is sleep. Except for Palomas and Zana, you all look horrible. No offense, Fig."

Palomas beamed while Fig shrugged, stifling a yawn.

"General Estrago, can you have us all excused from class today?"

General Estrago grunted in the affirmative.

"Good. Masay, since you're rested, go with General Estrago and scout the hangar bays with bipod transports. If we want to avoid the jungle and the wild beasts, we'll need to find a way to hijack a transport."

Masay smiled, clearly itching to move as his leg vibrated up and down.

"The rest of you get some rest. We'll meet back in my room tonight. We have a lot to plan before the Director arrives."

Aidan paused and looked at each individual in the room. "It looks like we're going to join the rebellion."

I hope you'll join the JT Reader Club to get the latest freebies, discounts, and exclusives on upcoming stories and events.

The JT is for Johan Twiss. Not sure how to pronounce my first name? Just pretend you saw Han Solo from Star Wars and said, "Yo, Han. What's up?"

There, you've got it!

**Go to www.johantwiss.com
to join the club today!**

SENTINEL'S CHALLENGE OF THREE

I am Sentinel, dragleon, keeper of secrets and the guardian of Legacy. Now that you have finished this simulation, I give you a challenge of three, which if you do not complete, I shall be forced to devour you, causing you to repeat this simulation again.

1. Write a review of 5 stars or 4, to be seen in the land of Amazon for life evermore. If your review is a 1, 2 or 3, although it is sad, we must let it be.

2. Tell your coteries of this amazing book they must read. Tell them on Facebook, Goodreads and your Blog and Twitter feeds. #iamsleepless

3. There is one more task that you must seek. Go to the next page and read the first chapter of book two, for it is a sneak peek.

SNEAK PEEK BOOK 2

I AM SLEEPLESS

THE HUNTRESS

CHAPTER 1: THE RACE

Before the Splicers returned, the ambassadors of Ethos and Hashmeer were locked in an arms race of deadly proportions. It had only been seventy-three years since we colonized the Univi system, and already we sat at the brink of war between our own people. We escaped the destruction of the Splicer War on Justus, only to return to the work of death like a kangadog to its vomit.

—Doctor T.M. Omori,
Man's Quest for Destruction: A Case for the Prime Initiative

I DIOTS! Your failure just earned each of you a spot on the front lines of Omori! Because of your foolishness, the Pit is no more. You were supposed to destroy the triplets from the programming, not destroy the programming itself!"

Director Tuskin fumed as he paced around the room housing the Advanced Programming Unit (APU). How had it all gone so wrong? He had lost the greatest technological advancement of the last two hundred years. The virtual world of the Pit was gone.

From the corner of the room a defiant human stood from his chair and spoke.

"This is not our fault. It is yours. You forced us to this outcome," he said, his voice starting to rise. "You forced us to work for you and forced this decision to attack the Pit! Your pride is your weakness. You have led this people into ruin continu-"

With a flash of vigori speed, the Director raced to the human, switched to a lug and grabbed the man by the throat, squeezing ever so slightly as he lifted the human programmer into the air with one hand.

"Your legs are *your* weakness!" Director Tuskin barked. "You dare stand to defy me?"

The Director threw the human to the ground, then changed to an agulator, floating in the air above the man. The human programmer rubbed his throat with one hand and raised his other in the air toward the Director, pleading for mercy.

Director Tuskin simply nodded his approval, his face covered by a white agulator mask. "Yes. Cower before me, *human*. You foolish man. You are the very one I am trying to protect from the Splicer invasion, and yet you defy me!"

The man tried to speak, but could only wheeze in deep breaths through his bruised throat.

"Be thankful I am a merciful ruler," the Director continued. "Instead of killing you, I will alleviate you of *your weakness.*"

The Director crashed down like a meteor on top of the man's legs. The man shrieked in pain and horror, struggling to breathe as the Director stood on his crushed legs.

"Take them all away!" the Director yelled to the guards in the room. "These worthless programmers are no longer part of the APU!"

The defiant human hyperventilated, going into shock. "You…will be…our undoing," he wheezed between hurried breaths.

That may be, the Director thought, watching as a guard dragged the man away. *But I'm also your only hope.*

***

"Welcome to the final trial of the Mount Fegorio complex," bellowed Director Tuskin through an amplified speaker system.

This was the first time the Director had made a public appearance in years, causing a combination of fear and excitement to run through those in attendance. Hundreds of prime cadets, master instructors, and the Mount Fegorio staff all cheered in wild anticipation while sitting snugly in stadium seats, freshly cut into the black wall in the cone of the dormant volcano. At the request of the Director, local prime peace officers from Vapor City were also in attendance. Four squadrons of trained lugs, agulators and mek peace officers filled the remaining seats to capacity.

Near the rim of the volcano, perched high above the cheering crowd, Director Tuskin stood atop an intricately carved black balcony jutting out from the volcanic wall. Wearing a brilliant white uniform of the Ethos Military, a white agulator mask, and a white cape, his form stood out like a shining beacon against the backdrop of black rock.

His exposed skin was the rich gold complexion of a lug, while his long red vigori hair spread out across his shoulders like wildfire. If one was close enough, they would have seen dark, brown eidetic eyes through the clear goggles of the agulator mask.

But no one was that close. They were all kept at a distance from the Director. No one was allowed near their supreme leader—no one, except General Estrago, the highest ranking master instructor at Mount Fegorio, and Captain Solsti, the second ranking master.

But Aidan did not have to be close to see the Director clearly. Focusing his vibruntcy, he saw every detail of their leader—a man they feared, and a man they planned to escape from.

Could he really be immortal? Aidan thought as he focused his vibruntcy on the Director high above them. There was a prick in the back of his mind telling him that something wasn't quite right with the leader standing high above them. He wasn't sure what it was, but something was off.

Aidan watched as his friend and mentor, General Estrago, sat in a black chair to the right of Director Tuskin, looking warily over the balcony ledge. Aidan knew the large eidetic was not particularly fond of heights, and worried what it was doing to the man's weak heart.

To the left of the Director sat Captain Solsti, whose calm presence, even from afar, helped Aidan to still his pounding heart.

But as Aidan took in the volcano's expansive cone, and the cheering grew louder, he felt his head begin to spin in circles. He looked at the Director's balcony far above and shuddered.

This is the real Pit, he thought. *No simulations this time.*

Aidan shuffled his feet on the black dirt and loose rocks that made up the floor of the volcano's cone. Palomas, Fig, and Masay huddled close around him. At twelve years old, they were the youngest coterie in the trial finals, as well as the smallest coterie, with only four members.

A few paces to their left, the nine fifteen-year cadets glared at them. Aidan could feel the malice seething from their leader, Kara. The female agulator hated Aidan with a passion. She hated him for beating her coterie in their first trial against each other, and blamed Aidan for ruining her relationship with Dixon—her now ex-boyfriend.

To Aidan's right was the large sixteen-year coterie, with ten soon-to-graduate seniors. Dixon and Zana led the group. Dixon gave Aidan a slight nod of encouragement, while Zana gave him three thumbs up with the three left hands on her mek suit.

Though Dixon and Zana were in the sixteen-year coterie, their recent adventures with Aidan in Sim 299 had turned them from enemies to battle comrades and fast friends. Aidan depended on their help if he and his coterie were to escape undetected.

Aidan returned a weak smile to Zana, but it quickly faded when he caught a glimpse of a group of prime peace officers in the background. They were stationed together in a block of seats near an exit. One of them in particular grabbed his attention. She wore distinctive purple armor, a full helmet, and a cloak that hung across her back.

It can't be, Aidan thought. *She's more of a legend than the Director himself.*

But even as Aidan disputed the idea, he knew it had to be her—Sheva, the Director's High Huntress.

Oh, man. This complicates things.

The Huntress seemed to be staring at him through her shielded helmet—or so it felt—and a hard, cold lump formed in Aidan's throat. He held her gaze for a moment, out of a mixture of curiosity and fear, before breaking away as the crowd began to hush.

From high above in his balcony, Director Tuskin raised a white-gloved hand into the air. All movement ceased and the volcano fell silent.

"This is a special and unique event. Today marks the two hundred and thirtieth year of the Splicer War. We have lost many brothers and sisters in this effort. It is the reason young primes are pushed to develop their abilities and are trained since childhood. Today also marks the first live trial between coteries—the beginning of a new age in our training process.

"These three coteries, the twelve-year, the fifteen-year and the sixteen-year, have tied as the top coteries to compete in the final trial. They will race against one another through extreme obstacles made to test their abilities. They must travel across the inner cone, down into the twisting heart of Mount Fegorio, and cross the finish line at the bottom exterior of the volcano's steep slopes."

The crowd went wild with anticipation. Director Tuskin allowed them to continue cheering for another moment before raising his hand once more to still the crowd.

"Since this is a live trial with greater dangers, the reward is equally greater. The winner of the final trial will receive a guaranteed officership in the Ethos Army and a maximum land grant of 3,000 acres in the fertile Western Isles."

An audible gasp rolled through the audience. Becoming an officer was indeed a high honor; but a land grant—in the Western Isles of all places—was a kingly reward.

"Your own Captain Solsti will signal the start of the race. May the best coterie win."

Director Tuskin nodded to Captain Solsti, who arose, carrying a long white handkerchief in her slender green hand.

Though she was blind, her vibrunt gift allowed her to see clearly through sound waves as she stood precariously close to the edge of the balcony. She raised the handkerchief in the air with her outstretched hand, and paused.

Aidan stretched his vibruntcy to zoom in on his instructor, and was surprised when Captain Solsti turned her head in his direction and smiled. It was the same calm, peaceful, yet determined smile she had given him many times as his tutor. After being taught by her in the ways of vibruntcy for nearly his whole life, he wondered if this was the last time he would see her smile. The thought pained him.

A few long seconds passed, and Captain Solsti dipped her head to him, then released the handkerchief.

Aidan found himself entranced as the soft white piece of cloth fell, billowing in the air against the black rock walls. He watched it flutter and swirl in the breeze until it landed gracefully on the dark ground. The race had begun.

ACKNOWLEDGMENTS

First and foremost, I must acknowledge my talented, patient, and beautiful wife, Adrienne. Not only does she act as my sounding board for the random ideas I share at all hours of the day, but she is my alpha reader, she is my beta reader, she is my first-pass editor, and she also happens to be my interior sketch artist. Basically, she is amazing and I love her.

This book would not be nearly as readable without the great work done by my editor, Heather Monson. Without her expert feedback and grammar/spelling edits, all y'all were fixin' to see my true southern roots and lack of punctuatianations void of those there commas and plentiful with them wayward's apostrophe's'. Thank you for all your improvements, Heather.

The magnificent cover artwork was created by the talented Sky Young, a professional animator, and friend, that went above and beyond in his research, preparation, and dedication to create the engaging cover you see today. Thank you, Sky.

Finally, I want to give a big shout-out to all of the beta readers that took time to read the pre-edited draft of this book and gave me detailed and brilliant feedback. Your insights and support helped improve this story ten-fold. So to Kent Meyers and Ken Meyers (my proof-readers extraordinaire), Renee Hirsch, Rachel Derenthal, Sean Derenthal, Steve Meyers, Hannah Peterson, Sarah Peterson, Nicole Kaimori, Arial Nometsiku, Aaron Grant, and Devora Burger, I give you a wholehearted thank you.

ABOUT THE AUTHOR

Dear Brilliant Reader,

Thank you for your interest in my books, and I hope you enjoyed reading *I Am Sleepless: Sim 299*.

I am passionate about writing clean science fiction and fantasy stories that are exciting and suitable for tweens, teens and adults alike.

Have a question? Complaint? Want to send me suitcases full of money in small denominations or a gift card to the Cheesecake Factory? Simply reach out to me at my website, Facebook, or Twitter pages.

www.johantwiss.com

www.facebook.com/JohanTwiss

www.twitter.com/JohanTwiss

If you'd like to schedule a free school visit, or video call with your book club, send me a message via my contact page at www.johantwiss.com/contact.html.

Lastly, I want to ask you for a favor. If you enjoyed reading this book, please leave a review for it on Amazon.com. Your reviews help new readers decide to give my books a try, for which I am thankful.

All the best,

Johan

OTHER BOOKS BY JOHAN TWISS

I Am Sleepless: Sim 299 (Book 1)

I Am Sleepless: The Huntress (Book 2)

I Am Sleepless: Traitors (Book 3)

I Am Sleepless: The Dark Throne (Book 4)

4 Years Trapped in My Mind Palace

The Fourth Law of Kanaloa

30 Red Dresses

When Sister Soul Stole the Blues

Made in the USA
Monee, IL
07 March 2024